BLOODWORK

BLOODWORK

THE NEW RUGGED CROSS

A NOVEL BY
HENRY JOSEPH

GIBBS-SMITH PUBLISHER

First Edition

95 94   10 9 8 7 6 5 4 3 2 1

This is a Peregrine Smith Book, published by
Gibbs Smith, Publisher
P.O. Box 667
Layton, Utah 84041

Book design by Clane Graves and Christopher Graves
Cover art by Cary Henrie
Lynda Sessions, Editor
Nikki Hansen, Editor
Dawn Valentine Hadlock, Editor
Printed and bound in the United States of America

Library of Congress Cataloging-in-Publication Data
Joseph, Henry, 1948-
        Bloodwork: the new rugged cross/ by Henry Joseph.
                p.   cm.
        ISBN 0-87905-628-2
        1. Drug traffic--Georgia--Fiction. 2. Murder--Georgia--Fiction.
I. Title.
PS3560 .07728B58   1994
813' .54--dc20   93-47158
                                                         CIP

For my mother, who prayed for a change;

and my father, who did not live to see it.

On a hill far away stood an old rugged cross,

The emblem of suffering and shame;

And I love that old cross where the dearest and best

For a world of lost sinners was slain.

So I'll cherish the old rugged cross,

till my trophies at last I lay down;

I will cling to the old rugged cross,

And exchange it someday for a crown.

From The Old Rugged Cross,

a hymn by George Bennard

CHAPTER 1

On a clear mid-October Wednesday afternoon, Lucius O'Dell flew directly into a setting sun so brilliant that he was momentarily blinded as he passed over Blackjack Mountain, in extreme west Georgia. By the time his eyes readjusted, he had crossed the Alabama border. With great disappointment, he banked the chopper hard to the right. When he had come about almost 180 degrees, he saw the skyline of the city of Atlanta seventy miles away. A feeling of failure swept over Lucius as he thought of returning empty-handed. Only two flying days remained in the season, and although he had found numerous small patches and three good-sized fields of marijuana, none of them had met the requirements of Reverend Clyde Causey. While technically he worked for the State of Georgia in the Marijuana Eradication Program, Lucius's only true concern was the secret mission that he was performing for Reverend Clyde. Reverend Clyde had stopped the flashbacks that had plagued Lucius for twenty-one years. Lucius considered Reverend Clyde to be his personal savior.

Lucius decided to call the Carroll County Sheriff's deputies on the ground and sign out for the day. He saw the first plant as he was reaching for the radio mike. Then his practiced eye picked out the long irregular rows along either side of the small creek that cut through the middle of a narrow valley nestled between two steep ridges. The entire valley appeared to have been clear-cut and replanted in pines that had now reached a height of eight to ten feet. In this near perfect cover, Lucius counted roughly five hundred mature marijuana plants so heavily laden with flowers that the tops of the plants had fallen over, nearly touching the ground.

A dead-end, two-rut logging road afforded the only access to the valley, which was situated one-half mile from the nearest house in any direction. Carefully, Lucius marked the location on his county road map and pressed the button on the mike.

"Eagle Eyes to Foxhound. Do you copy?"

"Roger that, Eagle Eyes," answered a member of the ground crew.

"I'm taking it home, Foxhound. See you at 0800 hours tomorrow at Carrollton Regional."

"10-4, Eagle Eyes."

Lucius felt a surpassing joy well up within him as he settled in for the forty minute flight back to Atlanta. For the first time all day, he became aware of the Joseph's coat of color that the fall foliage radiated below him. This is it, he thought. This will prove my loyalty to Reverend Clyde. Now, I'll be able to be closer to him— maybe even move up to the church's mountain camp.

A vague question formed in his mind regarding the reason for his mission. Before the question had time to take root, it was expunged by his absolute faith in Reverend Clyde. For the first time he felt good about the prospect of reporting to Clint DuBois.

***

Clint DuBois walked into the Vietnamese restaurant on the corner of Peachtree and Tenth Street at 7:45. He liked to arrive early for his meetings with Little Lulu, the private name he used for Lucius O'Dell. He felt about being among the Vietnamese the way that he imagined deer hunters felt about being close to their prey outside of hunting season. A certain kinship.

Mrs. Ky, the fifty-year-old proprietor, felt a chill when she saw him enter. She had seen more than a few of his kind in her time. His kind did not have thousand-yard stares. His kind did not have eyes dead from seeing too much. His eyes burned with a cold fire that told her that he had not seen enough death. That he would never see enough death.

Mrs. Ky watched him approach her, as he did each time he came. His tall, lean body glided stealthily toward her in a way that told her that he had never left the jungle. That he would never leave the jungle. She took in his close-cropped, coal-black hair that had not even one fleck of grey and knew that he had never known a worry. She appraised his totally composed face, framed by a blue-black beard so heavy that, in spite of the close shave, it threatened to explode in growth like some jungle creeper and ensnare everything around it. She avoided the onyx eyes by looking at a spot on the wall just over his right shoulder, wondering as she did so how many people had left this world gazing into those eyes.

"Good evening, Mrs. Ky," said DuBois.

Mrs. Ky nodded and gestured toward a table in the back right corner. She had never uttered a word to him. Would never speak to him. With a slight movement of her head, she conveyed an order for one of the waiters to attend him.

DuBois refused a menu and ordered a Ching Tao

beer. He had no intention of eating with Little Lulu. His reason for meeting the little man here was simple. Being among the Vietnamese made Lucius very nervous and therefore more vulnerable. DuBois liked to watch Little Lulu's moist blue eyes widen when he walked in. He liked to watch Lulu struggle to keep his composure and lose every time. DuBois knew Lulu's secret. He had listened in when Lulu had spilled his guts to Reverend Clyde about the village that he had destroyed by mistake with his gunship when he was high on LSD. DuBois marveled at the enormity of the man's regret, the depth of his conscience. He knew that when their time together came, Lucius's conscience would heighten his pleasure. And their time would come, of that he was sure.

When Lucius turned off Tenth street onto Peachtree, he felt a cold sweat break in his armpits. He stopped just outside the restaurant and took several deep breaths. Each inhalation brought to his nose the sour, acrid smell of his own fear. He felt confused by his fear as he did each time he met Clint. It didn't seem right that he should fear the man who had lead him to Reverend Clyde. When they had first met at the Vietnam Veterans' reunion up at Lake Allatoona, the previous Fourth of July, Lucius had felt drawn to Clint. Now, he felt drawn and repelled at the same time. Tonight will be different, he thought. Tonight I have good news.

Lucius sat down across the table from Clint and attempted a smile that his tense facial muscles transformed into a grimace.

"I think I finally found it."

"Tell me about it," Clint said.

Lucius reached into his shirt pocket and withdrew

a folded sheet of paper on which he had drawn a map. As he reached across the table to hand it to Clint, the waiter appeared. Lucius hesitated, withdrew his hand a few inches and finally dropped the paper in the middle of the table.

"J-j-just H-h-hot tea," he stuttered.

Clint waited until the waiter had left and said, "Take it easy, Lucius. Take a deep breath and tell me what you found."

"Well, there's about five hundred plants, Clint. Big ones. I mean, not real tall, maybe eight or nine feet, but, well, they look like little Christmas trees. Real well developed. They're so heavy with bud that most of them are sagging over toward the ground. Best looking plants I've ever seen. Somebody really knew what they were doing."

"Tell me about the location."

"Well, there's a logging road off Highway 5 about halfway between Tyus and Bucktown. On your right, coming west from Tyus you'll see a burned-out country store, maybe three miles from Tyus. The logging road is the first road on the right after the store, maybe a half mile. The logging road leads into a little valley and dead-ends. The valley is flanked on either side by ridges that run parallel for maybe a quarter mile, then close in on each other. Kinda forms a box canyon. Anyway, when the road ends, about a hundred yards to your left, there's a creek. Turn right and you'll find the pot growing on either side of the creek for a couple a hundred yards."

"Are there any houses close enough for someone to observe traffic on the logging road?"

Lucius shook his head. "There's not a house on either side of Highway 5 for almost a mile in either direction. Plus, the road's down at the bottom of a hill so somebody would have to be right on top of you to see you entering or leaving. Just like you wanted."

"Not like I wanted. Like Reverend Clyde wanted. You remember that, Lucius."

Lucius nodded.

"Is there a gate on the logging road?"

"No."

"Any houses close to the backside of the valley?"

"There's not a house within a half mile or more."

"Just one more question, Lucius. Will that area be flown again?"

"No. Tomorrow we'll go up to North Carroll and into Haralson County. Shouldn't be anybody within twenty miles."

DuBois unfolded the sheet of paper and studied the map for half a minute. "Well, you've done real well, Lucius. The Reverend is going to be real proud of you."

Relieved, Lucius gave DuBois a beaming smile. "Well, guess I'll see you Sunday, huh?"

DuBois met Lucius's smile with a level, deadpan stare and said, "I almost forgot. Reverend Clyde thinks it might be a good idea if you didn't come around for a while."

DuBois's words hit Lucius like a hammer to the solar plexus. His heart raced and he had a hard time drawing a breath. "But-but-w-why? I mean when can . . . "

DuBois rose and leaned over the table. "Now, Lucius, the Reverend knows best. You know that. Don't you?"

"Yes, but I thought . . ."

"I'm sure it's just for a little while. I'll be in touch as

soon as the time is right."

Lucius looked up at DuBois with wet eyes and quivering lips. The look was so poignant and pain filled that it produced a small smile on DuBois's face.

Across the room, Mrs. Ky saw the smile on DuBois's face and fought the strong impulse to raise her hands in the gesture intended to ward off the evil eye.

CHAPTER 2

The first light of morning found Jack Lee gazing thoughtfully at the sweet complication sleeping peacefully beside him. Slightly parted curtains had admitted a thin ray of dull, white light that cast a one-inch beam across the unruly mane of deep auburn hair fanned out behind her head. Her hair shone with healthy radiance even in the low intensity light. From her slightly parted lips, a fragrance like freshly cut apples wafted upward to his face. He closed his eyes and inhaled the miracle of her sweet morning breath with wonder. Her name rolled through his mind. Deborah O'Hara. The thought emerged that he was too old, entirely unready for this. Yet, there it was. During their lovemaking the previous evening, she had made an act of surrender so complete that his heart had been captured in the very act of possessing her. Afterward, they needed no words to acknowledge that they had become bound, one to the other. She had drifted into a smiling sleep. He had lain awake all night clearing the rubble of his broken plans from his mind.

They had met three weeks ago to the day. Jack had recently emerged from three years of solitude. One month prior to his forty-second birthday, he had been found innocent of federal charges of conspiracy to import marijuana. The long and ugly trial had capped twenty years of a balls-to-the-wall outlaw career that had left him physically and emotionally burned out. He walked away from the Trade with a half million dollars cash and a serious case of spiritual bankruptcy.

For three years, Jack had lived in a small cabin atop a ridge in the hill country of west Georgia. The cabin was situated in the middle of twenty-five acres of hardwood forest and, with the exception of electricity and running water, offered none of the amenities of modern life. He spent his days reading, meditating, gardening, and walking. Walking in the surrounding woods became a passion that often consumed half of his waking hours. As his body responded to the exercise and clean living and his mind learned stillness in the two hours of meditation that he practiced daily, Jack slowly found a rhythm that, by the end of the first year, was to remain constant until the end of the third. Then, it was simply over. He was sitting on the deck of the cabin one morning after meditation when he realized that he was whole again.

The first thing that Jack did was drive over to Whitesburg to visit his old friend and partner, Jim Smiley, who lived in a sprawling house on the banks of the Chattahoochee River. Smiley was splitting logs on a loud, gas-powered splitter when Jack eased the old '56 Chevy Apache pickup down the long gravel driveway. As he walked toward Smiley, Jack caught sight of Marge, Smiley's wife, waving excitedly through the kitchen window. He put a finger to his lips and walked over to Smiley and tapped him on the shoulder.

Smiley whirled around and settled in a boxer's stance, left shoulder dipped slightly and hands up and ready. His battered face ran the gamut from anger to shock to pleasurable surprise in the space of a second.

"Goddamnit, Jack, you know I can't stand people comin' up behind me like that," Smiley said, his grey eyes flashing in a smile-creased face. "Jesus, man, is it finally over?"

"It's over," Jack said as he held out his arms.

Smiley sprang forward and threw his squat, powerful body into Jack with ferocity. Finally, Smiley released him and, simultaneously raising his body upward and pulling Jack's taller body downward, kissed him on the cheek.

"We've missed you Jack," Smiley said with emotion. "Damn if we haven't missed you."

"Good to see you, too, I think," Jack said, holding his ribs. "You on steroids now, or what?"

Smiley flexed, in a Mr. Universe pose, and gave Jack a slightly smug smile. "I still try to keep it tight. Come on in and say hey to Marge."

Jack grinned and shook his head as he followed the banty rooster of a man into the house. As a youngster, Smiley had fought sixty amateur fights as a welterweight, winning fifty-five. Jack had never seen him in the ring, but he had once seen him take out three mean-drunk sailors in quick succession in a Montego Bay bar. Each man had fallen before an onslaught of wicked hooks to the body followed by clock-cleaning uppercuts, once their heads had been involuntarily lowered into range. Smiley was the only man Jack had ever known who he seriously thought might be able to whip his weight in wildcats.

Marge, towering by three inches over her husband, said, "Have you come down from the mountain, Jack?"

"Yep," said Jack. "And this is your chance to be the

first woman to give me a hug in three years."

Jack was aware of her small-boned delicacy as they embraced. She pushed him back gently and said, "Let me take a look at you."

Marge was one of the rare people in this world who can smile without any facial movement whatsoever. At first glance, she appeared plain. After being around her for some time, most people found themselves thinking, with surprise, 'What a beauty she is! How come I never noticed that before?'

"Something good happened up there," she said after a full minute. "You know that I prayed for you."

"I knew, Marge," Jack said. "Sometimes I could feel you up there with me."

"Jesus, Marge," said Smiley. "Are we gonna ask the guy in, or what?"

"Oh, hush!" Marge said with good humor. "As you can see, Jack, nothing has changed around here. Come in. I'll make tea."

Jack felt a warm glow of pure affection for the couple as he followed them into the house. Their marriage of opposites was a piece of work the likes of which he had never seen. They were people he had ridden the river with and he was content to be with them.

They whiled away the morning and then they whiled away the afternoon as old friends tend to do after a long absence. They touched upon every subject of interest as the hours faded one into the other. Smiley had bought a Ranger bass boat and had opened a charter fishing service at nearby West Point Lake. Marge had continued to find time to write poetry, some of which had been published in state and regional poetry journals, in between her motherly and household duties. She was, Jack thought, the kind of woman who gives homemaking a good name. Jack learned that the children were doing well. Carson, their twelve-year-old son, was now in the sixth grade, a budding sportsman and fishing fanatic like his father. Laurie, their nine-year-old daughter, was in the third grade, a beautiful and serious girl who had begun to write precocious stories, the dark content of which gave her parents pause for worry.

Jack, for his part, tried to explain the measure of peace that he had found up on the ridge. Marge listened quietly with wistful smiles and slight nods of her head. Smiley, ever the man of action, interrupted periodically to express his incredulity. "Jesus, man. You! No booze. No dope. No women. Not even a TV or a fucking radio. Jeeesus!"

The waning of the sun dovetailed with the waning conversation. When Jack rose to announce his departure, Smiley popped his forehead lightly with the heel of his hand. "I almost forgot," he said. "Listen, man, we're having a little get-together here tomorrow. Coupla folks from Greenpeace are holding a Save-the-Chattahoochee rally. Gonna be lotsa folks, good food, music, the whole nine, man; we're gonna make a day of it. You oughta dig up some of that loot you've got stashed and make a donation. Either way, you're invited. Come on, I'll walk you to the truck."

When they reached the truck, Smiley said, "Let's walk for a minute. I got something I want to run by you."

They strolled along the river bank for a while. Smiley's head was down and his hands were jammed deeply into the pockets of his jeans. Smiley was thinking deeply, struggling for words.

The late September heat had finally broken. A light breeze carried cool, moist air from the dying river, which glowed golden and amber in the lowering sun. Jack watched swirls of mist play upon the water and waited for Smiley to speak.

Smiley stopped and looked out over the river. "They've almost killed it, Jack. When I built here fifteen years ago, we swam in it, ate the fish from it. Now, it's just one big sewage line. Everything south of Atlanta is dying. Open sores on the fish. Chemicals in there I can't even pronounce. I don't know, man. I'm thinking about selling out and moving up to North Carolina. Maybe up around Asheville. Build a house up in the mountains, dig in for the duration. You know?"

Jack looked at Smiley and nodded, aware that he was having difficulty broaching the real subject. "Come on, Smiley. What's on your mind?"

Smiley gave him a tight smile and scuffed his shoes into the riverbank. "Well, truth is, Jack, things have gotten tight. Real tight. I've kept my hand out of the Trade since the trial. Went out and bought a fancy bass rig. Hell, I haven't run a charter in a month. Did OK the first year. Then this recession set in and people just quit spending money. I know you've been out of touch but, well, it's tough all over. I've had nothing coming in for two years now and with the kids, the bills—just general living expenses—well, I'm just watching everything I've saved fly out the door."

"Look, Smiley. I'm flush. If you need a loan, just say so."

"Nah, I've still got a hundred grand in the kitty. What I'd like you to do, Jack, is help me sell my crop when it comes in."

"What the hell are you talking about, Smiley?"

"I put in a crop of herb, man. I got almost five hundred of the most beautiful plants you've ever seen. Pure Indica. Got the seeds from this Dutch seed catalog. Strain's called Oakland Indica. Heavy yield. I think I'm gonna have two hundred pounds of pure sinse, maybe two-fifty."

"Sorry, Smiley. What I said three years ago still stands. I'm out of it."

"Yeah, I figured you'd say that, but listen to me. This shit's going for twenty-five hundred a pound wholesale. I'll take fifteen, I'm not greedy. You could tack on five for yourself and still come in five under the market."

"I don't want five, Smiley. I don't want a penny. I'm out of it. Comprende?"

"Listen, Jack, you were always the one with the connections. I ran the boats. I was good at that. When the shit came down, I personally drove that last cigarette boat back from Belize. Without that, neither one of us woulda walked away with shit. Between the lawyers and what it took to keep the boys happy, we wouldn't have had shit. I could sell this shit over time in tens and twenties, but I was hoping I wouldn't have to get my name in the street. Those guys you know, hell, they'd knock this out in one shot. Nice and clean. I can get over on this, Jack. You don't want to be around, fine. Introduce me to those dudes from New York. I'll take care of the rest. Then I'm out of it, too. For good. How 'bout it Jack?"

Jack was silent for a long moment. Smiley braced himself for the inevitable angry outburst that occurred when he put Jack on the spot. Jack, too, unconsciously waited for the surge of anger. Instead of anger, a mental picture arose in Jack's mind. Flashing blue lights. Men, uniformed and plainclothed, with guns drawn. Smiley, hands cuffed behind his back, being led to a squad car. Marge, flanked by her children, crying, close to the edge. When the picture faded, Jack looked at Smiley's expectant face and saw a desperation that he did not understand. His reason informed him that if he didn't help Smiley, there was every probability that the picture he had seen would come true. "OK, Smiley, when are you coming out of the ground?"

Smiley slapped his hands together explosively and said, "All right! Three weeks from today, Jack. Friday the nineteenth. I'll be cured, cleaned, and packaged in two weeks at the outside. I appreciate it, man, really."

"Look, Smiley. I'll make a call. Offer your shit at two. If there's interest, fine, I'll put you together with the people. Then I walk away. I don't want a thing from it. And I want you to never, ever ask me anything like this again. You understand?"

"Understood, Jack. You won't regret it."

CHAPTER 3

Jack drove back to Smiley's the next morning and found row upon row of cars and pickups parked in the spacious back yard. He had not expected to see such a large crowd at the Save-the-Chattahoochee rally and toyed momentarily with the idea of leaving until he remembered the envelope in his pocket. Smiley came trotting up to him as he approached the house.

"Hey, man, thought you weren't gonna make it."

"I almost left when I saw the size of the crowd. You think this Greenpeace outfit can make a difference in this Save-the-Hooch campaign?"

"Damn straight, buddy. Check the size of this crowd. This is the biggest event we've had since the downstreamers first started trying to organize to fight those cocksuckers in Atlanta."

"Downstreamers?"

"Yeah, you know, people living downstream of Atlanta. That's what we call ourselves. Come on, there's a lady from Greenpeace speaking now, a marine biologist."

When they started down the slope to the riverbank, Jack saw about a hundred and fifty people seated haphazardly on the chairs and blankets. Before them stood a tall, athletic woman with a cascading tangle of curly auburn hair with life of its own. She spoke in a clear, deep voice that carried easily to the spot where Jack had stopped some twenty feet from the back of the crowd. Her hands moved in graceful, flowing motions that reminded Jack of the mudras employed in classical Indian dance. The statistics that she cited, the offending companies and corporations that she listed, the strategies that she outlined were all lost on Jack, who heard the voice, but not the words as he stood nearly mesmerized by her flowing hands. When the hands became still and the voice fell silent, Jack looked up to her face and found that she was looking directly at him. A smile composed of pure light appeared on her face and snapped him out of his reverie. He returned her smile, aware that several heads in the audience had turned in his direction.

Jack felt a poke in his ribs and turned to a grinning Smiley. "Like an introduction?" Smiley asked.

They weaved their way through a crowd lining up at the tables designated for donations and water-testing kits. When Jack saw that the woman was accepting donations, he told Smiley that he would introduce himself and moved to the back of the line. He observed her as she interacted with each person in the slow-moving line. The auburn curls framed a strong face. She had a good, high forehead below which a pair of hazel eyes with the hint of the feline about them apprehended the world at a glance. The long, straight nose worked nicely with the wide-angled, high cheekbones, pink, full-lipped mouth, and lightly dimpled chin. She had a swimmer's body: broad shoulders, medium breasts that lifted her Greenpeace T-shirt without any support, short waist, long legs, and a high, compact derriere straight out of central casting. There did not appear to be an excess ounce of fat on her five-nine frame.

When Jack finally reached her, she held out her hand and said, "Ah, Mr. Jack Lee. I'm Deborah O'Hara."

Jack shook her warm, dry hand. He held onto her hand for a few seconds, noting the firmness of her grip. "Uh-oh," he said. "Marge has been playing with her voodoo dolls."

"I got that distinct impression when Marge told me you might be here today. She's been telling me about her friend, the mysterious man of the mountain, for over a year now."

Jack laughed. "That woman has been trying to marry me off for over ten years now."

"Fear not, sir, you're safe with me."

"In that case, are you free for lunch?"

"I'm free—period, Mr. Lee, and, yes, I would like that. Are you a veggie?"

Jack nodded.

"In that case, I'll have whatever you're having. I'll join you as soon as I've counted this money, which shouldn't take long from the looks of it."

A predominance of one dollar bills along with a sprinkling of fives, tens, and the odd twenty half filled the small tin bucket. Jack reached into his back pocket and produced a fairly thick envelope. "I almost forgot. First, though, does the money collected here go specifically for this Hooch fund or into the general coffers?"

"These donations are solely for the river project. Guaranteed. I can explain disbursement procedures over lunch if you like."

"Anonymity guaranteed, too?"

"Absolutely."

"In that case, have fun," said Jack as he tossed the envelope into the bucket. "I'm off to the vittles."

Fifteen minutes later she found Jack sitting under a large oak beside two trays containing spiced dal soup, brown rice, vegetable casserole, and tossed salad.

"Jesus H. Christ, Jack!" she said, a flush upon her cheeks.

Jack looked at her mildly and shrugged his shoulders.

"Why $9,999?"

"Well, I haven't been much of a citizen lately and I love this river."

"No, I mean why that precise amount?"

"Is that a rhetorical question?"

"You know damn well what kind of question that is."

"Any cash transaction of $10,000 or more must, by law, be reported to the IRS. I'd just as soon skip that part. If you want to know more than that, you'll have to come home with me."

She threw back her head and laughed. "You are truly a cheeky bastard. Give me one good reason why I should."

"I'll give you two. Something happened when I saw you. I think something happened to you, too."

"And what happened to you, Jack?"

"My heart turned over."

"Mine too, Jack. Lord help us, my heart turned over too."

***

Jack rolled carefully onto his back and watched motes of dust float into the brightening light. My heart is still turning over, he thought. If she won't come with me, I will stay with her.

They had driven from Smiley's up to his cabin on the ridge. For three days they had made love, baring their souls to each other and trading secrets like thieves in the night. They found that they fit each other like favorite clothes. The idea of separation seemed so ludicrous as to be unmentionable.

When Deborah had to return to work, Jack moved into her apartment in Atlanta. After two weeks of living in the moment, they began to think about the future. She felt committed to her work. Jack wanted to buy round-the-world airline tickets and set off on a grand wander. He had originally thought of the trip as a solo venture, the perfect counterpoint to the three years of rootedness. Now, the idea of leaving without her had lost all appeal. After days of tiptoeing around the issue, they had agreed to get away for a weekend and come to some sort of decision. Smiley had given them the keys to his parents' house on Lake Burton, in the northeast Georgia mountains, and they had driven up late Friday afternoon.

Jack eased from the bed and slipped into a long flannel robe. The stairs felt cold to his bare feet as he moved quietly down the staircase. After he had lit a small gas space heater and put on water for tea, he threw back the living room curtains and was greeted by a saffron sun rising over the mountains.

When the Ceylon tea had steeped, Jack poured a large cup, added honey and cream, and walked out onto the deck. The rising sun had cast its light upon the waters of the small cove, transforming the dancing water into a molten pool of yellow gold. A light breeze set the colorful autumn leaves atremble, creating a constant sibilant hiss. Jack turned his face into the warmth of the sun and closed his eyes. With the weight of decision lifted from him, he felt almost intangibly light, a creature made of air. I will stand here in this light and count my blessings, he thought. And I will be content.

CHAPTER 4

Courtney Fowler made the decision over a dessert of chocolate crepes, coffee, and brandy at Dante's Down the Hatch. Her doubts about Tom Doyle had begun to unravel during a long, romantic dinner at the Ritz-Carlton in Buckhead. For some time, she had suspected that Tom's goal was to lure her away from her job at *Atlanta Today,* in order to secure her services for the news department at the local network affiliate where he was the lead anchor. Those doubts had caused her to keep herself emotionally and physically distanced from him. She had assumed that when she signed her new contract at *AT,* he would gracefully fade from the scene. To her surprise and delight, he had intensified his wooing of her. The flowers, the elegant dinners, the intimate slow dancing had all been a welcomed relief from the mindless cocaine- and alcohol-fueled social scene that she had drifted into out of loneliness and boredom. Tonight, I will surprise you, she thought.

During the ride home, Courtney reflected on the past year. She had been nominated for a Pulitzer for her series of investigative reports concerning the bribing of local legislators by Japanese business interests, the first such honor ever given to a reporter from a local, alternative publication. That had led to her inclusion in a number of local and regionally televised discussion groups focusing on the selling of the South to foreign interest groups. Her incisive commentary, smooth delivery, and

stunning looks had combined to make her an instanta-
neous hot property. After her appearance on McNeil-
Lehrer, offers from both print and electronic media
began to pour in.

Meanwhile, circulation at *AT* jumped from one
hundred thousand to one hundred fifty thousand.
Advertising revenues had doubled, allowing the paper to
move from weekly to bi-weekly publication. Finally, and
foremost in Courtney's decision to remain at *AT*, the par-
ent corporation had released funding for *AT's* purchase
of a small, financially-strapped independent TV station
with a broadcast range over seventy-five miles.

When the president of *Atlanta Today* had called
her in and offered her a package that included one percent ownership of the company, $159,000 per year plus
liberal expenses, a thirty-minute weekly exposé TV program complete with mobile broadcast unit and sound
and video personnel, and a continuing column in the
newspaper, she had signed a five-year contract on the
spot.

And now this, she thought, as they reached the end
of the driveway of her newly renovated house in
Brookhaven. The warm feeling for Tom had reached a
part of her that had been closed off for so long that she
had ceased to be aware of it. This feeling imparted a
deeper meaning to the rest of her life, a balance that had
been sorely lacking. When he leaned toward her, she
turned to him and felt a sharp tingling in her belly.

"It's been a lovely evening," he said. "Actually,
more than lovely. It has been perfect."

She studied his face for a moment. He was handsome in a craggy sort of way. His dark eyes hinted at

experience beyond his forty-five years. Courtney assumed that he had known many women during his ten-year stint as a network foreign correspondent. She read desire in his face and loved him for not having pressed that desire upon her in any way. Leaning closer to him, she simultaneously turned the ignition key off with her right hand and pulled his face down to hers with the left. She brushed his lips lightly with her own and then kissed him. Kissed him deep and true. When they separated, she saw upon his face the look that she had hoped for. The look spoke of deep hunger and arousal.

"The evening is only over if you want it to be," she said. "I would like for you to stay."

They walked arm in arm toward the front door. She saw the envelope taped to the door when she reached the top step. The typewritten words MS. FOWLER—URGENT announced the front of it.

Feelings of excitement, disappointment, and a vague foreboding arose in her as she reached for the envelope and opened it. Inside, there was a single sheet of paper with a map at the top end and a terse statement typed across the bottom. The map outlined directions from Atlanta to Douglasville via Interstate 20 West, then south on State Highway 5 for exactly 47.3 miles. An "X" marked the entrance of a road on the right just past the drawing of a building with the words BURNED OUT COUNTRY STORE printed beside it in a childlike hand. An arrow, with the words LOGGING ROAD—GO THREE HUNDRED YARDS printed along the shaft, pointed to another "X" down the road. The words FOR THE STORY OF YOUR LIFE BE HERE AT SUNRISE

SATURDAY were typed across the bottom of the page.

Courtney felt the reporter in her stir, felt the instinct that she always followed becoming engaged. The word "no" escaped her lips, barely audible. A war of conflicting emotions and thoughts erupted in her mind and heart. Her desire to be with Tom joined forces with her rational mind. Don't be a fool, reason and desire told her. This is some sort of prank. Don't lose this moment. Instinct, coming fully awake, yawned and said, "OK, bitch, let's get to work."

"Is there a problem?" Tom asked.

"Something has come up. Work. I'm terribly sorry, Tom. Can I offer you a rain check?"

The look of concern faded from Tom's face and was replaced by the deflated look of disappointment. He recovered quickly and gave her a wry, rueful grin. "Work. I understand only too well." He kissed her on the forehead and said, "Rain check accepted."

She stood on the porch and watched his car disappear into the night, then checked her wristwatch. Five and a half hours till sunrise, she thought. Then she entered the house and set about the business of ruining the night for her sound and video people.

CHAPTER 5

Deborah awoke and, finding herself alone, stretched her limbs luxuriously along the width and length of the bed. Various minor aches and soreness announced themselves as she did so, triggering a flood of memories from the previous night's lovemaking. She smiled and placed her hand lightly over her bruised pudenda, from which a vague, dull ache emanated. The recollection of a certain moment brought a blush to her face. She reached up with both hands and upon feeling her hot cheeks laughed aloud.

She closed her eyes and formed an image of him in her mind. Oh, Jack Lee, how I love you, she thought. How I love your long, lived-in face and your pale blue eyes. Your graying copper hair. Your strong, lean body that knows mine so well. The way I feel like a giggling schoolgirl one moment and a wise courtesan the next. The way I feel connected as I've never felt before.

She hugged herself tightly and then lay very still. I'll go with him, she thought. I can take a year's sabbatical. I can take a lifetime if necessary.

When Deborah, fresh from her morning toilet, started down the stairs, she was greeted by the wafting aromas of brewing coffee and buckwheat pancakes. She found Jack tending a large pancake in a cast-iron skillet.

"Hungry?"

"Starved," she said, noting his puffy eyes. "Did you get any sleep?"

"During the night, no. I spent the night thinking. But I got up for sunrise and then crashed out on the couch for three hours."

"Gracious, what time is it?"

"Going on noon."

"Well, I must have done my thinking in my sleep because my decision was made when I opened my eyes."

"Mine was made before I finally closed mine."

"You first."

"No, ladies first."

Deborah laughed and picked up a pen and message tablet beside the telephone. She wrote briefly on a small sheet of paper, tore it off the pad and handed pen and paper to Jack.

"Write it out and we'll trade."

After they had traded and read each other's answers, they fell laughing into each other's arms.

"Looks like we'll have to treat this with the seriousness that it deserves," said Jack.

"How so?"

"Gotta coin?"

Deborah reached into the pocket of her jeans and produced a quarter.

"Flip it," said Jack. "Heads we travel, tails we stay."

She flipped the coin high, almost touching the ceiling. Spinning rapidly, it hit the throw rug in the middle of the kitchen floor, rolled on its edge for almost a complete circle, wobbled, and landed on its side.

"Looks like Christmas in the islands," Jack said. "Can you handle that?"

"I get first choice of islands?"

"You bet."

"In that case, you're on."

They spent a leisurely breakfast talking about places that each had always wanted to visit. Jack studied Deborah for any signs of misgiving and, finding none, was relieved. Deborah felt surprised by the intensity of the enthusiasm that she felt growing in her.

After breakfast, they decided to take a boat ride around the lake. Jack was shutting the door on the way out when the phone rang. Smiley, he thought, late again as usual. Smiley was supposed to have called at 10:00 to let him know that his harvest yesterday had gone smoothly.

When Jack picked up the receiver, he heard a woman sobbing before he could get it to his ear.

"Hello. Marge?"

"Oh, Jack. My god. My god. My god," Marge said in high wailing sobs.

"What's happened, Marge?"

"It's Smiley, Jack. On the TV."

Jack felt an old, familiar sinking feeling as he asked what channel she was watching.

"ATV, Jack, ATV. I can't talk anymore now," she said and then burst out into another bout of sobs.

Jack heard a click on the line. He ran to the door and threw it open.

"Deborah, what the hell is ATV?" he asked in a voice louder than he had intended and filled with a panic that he had not meant to betray.

"It's a new Atlanta station," Deborah shouted up from the dock. "Channel fifty-two. Why? What's going on?"

Without answering, Jack raced into the den where he found a twenty-seven inch Sony with the remote control changer on top. He hit the power button and prayed that the satellite dish accessed channel fifty-two clearly. When he punched fifty-two on the remote, Smiley came on the screen and time stopped.

Jack stared at the screen with horrible fascination. He felt his mind misfire, actually felt something like an electric shock in his head as he tried to comprehend the scene before him. Then, a chill passed through him, leaving him in a state of emotional suspension.

Smiley hung from a wooden cross, his hands and feet nailed to it by what appeared to be metal spikes of the same type used by mountain climbers. The cross stood in the middle of several marijuana plants. Smiley's head hung down and was covered by a woven crown of marijuana flowers. His ears had been cut off and twin streaks of blood ran down the wounds over each breast and down the length of his body. His body, clothed only in a pair of jockey shorts, was rigid and blue from exposure.

Jack was aware of gagging behind him. He heard Deborah run from the room then the sound of a slamming door and violent retching.

A beautiful woman with tears in her eyes came onto the screen and spoke into a handheld mike, standing before a backdrop of ten-foot pines. Jack found himself unable to tune in her words until the very end of her statement.

"This is Courtney Fowler, WATV News, reporting live from Carroll County."

CHAPTER 6

At 11:30 A.M. Saturday morning, Lucius O'Dell rose from the sweaty sheets of his bed and staggered to the living room of his small house on Los Angeles Avenue, just off North Highland. With shaking hands, he ripped the plastic facing away from the cardboard backing of two ten-milligram Valiums. Then he reached down and picked up a half-full jug of Gallo white port, popped the Valiums into his mouth, and washed them down with four deep swallows of wine. He stood there for a moment, weak-kneed, and fought a successful battle with his rising gorge. When he was satisfied that he would not throw up, he sat down heavily in his recliner, leaned back, and placed the jug between his legs.

Lucius had been drinking heavily and popping twice his usual dosage of Valium since Wednesday night, when Clint DuBois had told him that he was not to see Reverend Clyde for an unspecified period of time. That news had produced an almost debilitating anxiety in him along with the symptoms that foreshadowed the painful bouts of hallucinatory visions to which he was prone.

In 1969, while flying his last combat mission, Lucius had received an urgent radio order to proceed to and destroy a small village in the NLF-held region of the Mekong Delta. He was flying close combat support for the U.S. Ninth Division, which had been assigned the duty of "cleaning out" the area of VC under the terms of the Accelerated Pacification Campaign.

At a party the previous evening, Lucius had been given a tiny square of paper that contained 400 mikes of Sandoz LSD-25. He had also been given a copy of a Jimi Hendrix tape. When he arrived at the village, he was still experiencing mild hallucinations. The song "Purple Haze" was blaring from the speaker of his portable tape player.

Bright swirls of color played at his periphery as he hovered and set his angle of attack. When he disgorged his massive payload into the village, Lucius was stunned by the acid-enhanced visual display. As the smoke began to clear, he started a slow 360 around the perimeter. When the truth of the scene below him finally registered in his foggy brain, he vomited violently onto the controls.

The final body count had been 81 dead and 53 wounded. There was one survivor, a year-old baby girl found unhurt beneath the dead body of an aged Vietnamese woman. Among the dead and wounded, there were 108 children and 26 old women. The fact that his attack order had been based on faulty intelligence and was in no measure his own fault did nothing to dispel the horror that Lucius felt. A few months after his return to the states, he began to relive the experience, at first in dreams and then in episodes of waking hallucinations that sometimes lasted for as long as five minutes. The waking flashbacks were always preceded by a tingling in his extremities, a roaring noise in his ears, and a powerful metallic copper taste in his mouth.

Lucius felt relieved when he felt the numbing fingers of the Valium begin to massage his body. He had been aware since Wednesday night that the forces of hallucination were building in him, waiting for an unguarded moment to break through. He lifted the jug and took a long draught, then reached toward the table next to him and replaced the receiver on the telephone, which had been off the hook since Wednesday night. One Valium left, he thought. Time to call Doc Cole. He dialed a number and hung up on the first ring. I'll watch her first, he thought.

Lucius had fallen in love with Courtney Fowler the first time he saw her on television. Since that first time six months ago, he had not missed her noontime Saturday show even once. She was the first woman since his fiancée Jenny who had touched him so deeply. Things had fallen apart with Jenny shortly after he had returned from Nam, and as one year drifted into another, he had come to realize that he would never again know a real relationship with a woman. With Courtney, it was different. By loving her from a distance, he was able to experience a purity of emotion that could not be sullied by personal interaction. He had come to accept the limitations of his long distance affair and felt no yearning to know Courtney personally.

When Courtney's face came on the screen with tears in her eyes, against the backdrop of the forest, Lucius felt confused. He was accustomed to seeing her smiling face in a studio setting. When the man hanging on the cross came into view, Lucius felt totally baffled. Then he saw the marijuana plants and felt something seize up in his chest. He recognized the valley when the camera panned a slow, sweeping shot of the area behind the man on the cross. When Courtney gave the location off Highway 5 in Carroll County, Lucius screamed.

Clint DuBois turned onto Los Angeles Avenue just in time to see Lucius slam his front door, stagger across the front yard, open the door of his Toyota, and lurch drunkenly into the driver's seat. Clint started to block the Toyota with his van but, on impulse, drove on by and made a U-turn at the end of the block. The little bastard's already heard, he thought, as he followed the Toyota south on North Highland. Clint followed the weaving car to Ponce de Leon, where Lucius turned left and headed east at a high rate of speed. Little fucker's gonna get stopped before I can see where he's going, he thought. Clint gunned the van, momentarily lost sight of the Toyota, then picked it back up as it turned left on Clairmont. Two blocks down Clairmont, Clint saw the Toyota pull into the driveway of a two-storied brick house on the right. He noted the number on the mailbox and, finding no suitable place to park, began to cruise the neighborhood slowly.

CHAPTER 7

When the doorbell began to ring, Dr. Benjamin Cole, a psychiatrist, was in the act of penetrating sixteen-year-old Candice Miller, a former patient. When Doc Cole attempted to withdraw from her, Candy reached around him with her long arms, clutched his buttocks, and pulled him fiercely back into her.

"Come on, Doc, I'm hot for it. Forget the door."

Doc Cole looked into her wanton eyes and decided that she was right. In matters of sex, my dear, you are always right, he thought, as he began to find a slow rhythm. Candy had been one of his last legitimate patients. Her parents had brought the sexually precocious twelve-year-old to him, fearful that she suffered from nymphomania or worse. When two of Doc's patients, one male, one female, had brought malpractice charges against him for having sex with them during therapy, his clientele, Candy included, had disappeared. Doc Cole had managed to keep his license and to become a writing doctor, a purveyor of legal drugs to a burgeoning clientele of legal junkies. When Candy had showed up on his doorstep at the tender age of fifteen, one year beyond the purview of Georgia's liberal statutory laws, Doc Cole figured that he had nothing to lose, especially with regard to reputation.

Doc and Candy were down to the short strokes when a two-fisted barrage unleashed upon the front door and a high, wailing voice implored Doc to open up in the name of emergency. Doc fought free from the grasp of Candy, rose from the bed and leaned gasping against the bedroom wall. While catching his breath, Doc recognized the voice outside. Disgusted, he snatched a robe from the closet and marched to the front door.

The rebuke that Doc had prepared died in his throat when he flung the door open, confronted with the sight of Lucius. The pupils of Lucius's eyes were so dilated that only a slight circle of blue surrounded them. The whites of his eyes had turned neon red and tears rushed down his cheeks. He was babbling a word salad, the ingredients of which were lost on Doc Cole except for the words Judas, Reverend Clyde, Clint, and crucified.

Doc grabbed Lucius by the arm, led him forcibly to a chair, and pushed him down into it. When Candy, wrapped in a towel, appeared in the room, Lucius cried out "Oh, Courtney!" and stumbled toward her. Doc intercepted him, strong-armed him back into the chair, and hustled Candy back into the bedroom, where he instructed her to get dressed and leave by the back way, pronto.

Hippocrates whispered in one ear and Satan in the other as Doc Cole stood paralyzed in the hallway, wondering what to do. This guy is in the deep woods, he thought, prepsychotic. And I've been overprescribing Valium to him for over three years. Jesus, I don't need this.

Lucius regained a modicum of lucidity when Doc led him into the therapy room at the back of the house. Seeing this, Doc decided to adopt a slightly stern, professional demeanor.

"Now, Lucius, you know that this is highly irregular. In fact, this is totally unacceptable. What in the world happened that is so important that you couldn't wait until office hours on Monday?"

Lucius struggled for words and then fell apart. When his head fell forward, large teardrops splattered on his knees. His shoulders shook and quaked and a series of deep, primal sobs wracked his body. When the tremor had passed, Lucius lifted his head and revealed a face that looked, except for the tears and red eyes, eerily composed.

"They made me a Judas, Doc," he said in a flat monotone. "They crucified him and made me the Judas."

"Who crucified whom, Lucius?" Doc asked, his mind racing for a quick way to terminate the conversation and get Lucius out of his house.

"Reverend Clyde and Clint, I guess. I don't know who the guy was they crucified but they made me out the Judas. I trusted 'em Doc and they did me in."

"Have you been having hallucinations again, Lucius?"

"Not yet, but I can feel it coming on. I'm outa pills, Doc, and I need 'em real bad right now. That's why I had to come."

Doc Cole wondered if he could cut him off right then without creating a scene and decided that he couldn't. I'll write this last one and that's it, he thought.

"Have you been flying, Lucius?"

"Not since Wednesday when Clint told me I couldn't see Reverend Clyde. That's when I started feelin' it comin' back on me. Then when I saw Courtney on the TV this morning I kinda lost it."

I don't want to know about any of this, Doc thought. This guy is about to crash and burn.

"Now Lucius, I've warned you many times about mixing flying with medication, haven't I?"

"Sure, Doc. Look I need to get that script and go. I'm not feelin' so hot."

Doc wrote out a prescription for twenty-five Valium, non-refillable, and handed it to Lucius. He marveled over the fact that the man in front of him had managed to keep it together for very long, particularly while flying. But, it's over now, Lucius; you're not going to make it.

"I'm afraid that this is going to have to be your last visit, Lucius. I think you are going to require more help than I'm qualified to give you. Perhaps it is time for you to seek out a doctor who specializes in Delayed Stress Syndrome. I suggest that you try the V.A. hospital. They have some excellent people on staff there."

Lucius turned a crestfallen gaze upon Doc Cole and said. "You, too, huh Doc?" Then he stood and walked slowly out of the house.

CHAPTER 8

Jack awoke Sunday morning and experienced a brief state of forgetful grace before the memory of Smiley's death flooded his consciousness producing a prolonged sinking sensation. When he finally hit bottom, he lay very still and attempted to make some sense of yesterday's events. He felt his brain misfiring, felt his thoughts try to bridge the synapses and, failing, fall into the chasms of lost thought.

He and Deborah had driven back to Atlanta the day before in near total silence. Jack felt like he had been fetched a great clout by some malevolent god and struck incomprehensibly dumb. The shock had turned Deborah's insides to water, and they had had to make numerous stops to accommodate her bouts of vomiting and diarrhea.

Jack had called Marge from Deborah's apartment and found out that the police were searching Marge's house at that very moment. Jack and Marge had decided that Jack would wait until Sunday morning to visit her.

Jack felt a stirring beside him and then a cold hand slipping into his. He accepted Deborah into his arms, feeling hollow as he did so. He realized that she was crying softly and attempted to comfort her, finding in the process that he had no comfort to give.

"What time do you have to go?" she asked

"I should leave now."

"Are you sure I couldn't be of help out there?"

"She was very clear about wanting to be alone. I have that same sort of feeling. I'm only planning to stay with her as long as necessary, then drive out to the ridge. See if I can sort all of this out."

"I'll be here if you need anything. Tell Marge that, too."

"I'll tell her. It may be a while before I'm back in touch. I'll call when I've figured out what to do about all of this."

"What do you mean, what to do about all of this, Jack?"

"I don't know."

Jack drove the sixty miles to Marge's with a feeling of dread anticipation and the nagging thought that something was wrong in the front page story of the *Atlanta Journal Constitution*. He had stopped at a convenience store for coffee and scanned the story as he drank it. About ten miles from Whitesburg, he remembered his conversation by the river with Smiley. Smiley had told him that he had nearly five hundred plants. The story in the paper had quoted Sheriff's Deputies as saying that two hundred plants had been found. Courtney Fowler, the reporter, had been the first one on the scene, which seemed to rule out the not uncommon occurrence of the police under-reporting a crop and keeping part of it for themselves. Maybe Smiley had already harvested part of the crop before . . . before what? Jack thought. His mind balked at the idea of what had happened to Smiley. How it had happened.

Laurie, Smiley and Marge's daughter, was in the yard when Jack pulled up. Jack felt at a total loss for words as he approached her and looked into her dark-eyed, brooding face.

"They crucified my daddy, Uncle Jack. Just like Jesus."

Before Jack could respond, the young girl turned and raced away toward the river. Her words penetrated Jack and heightened the feelings of dislocation and unreality that had plagued him since Smiley had appeared on the screen at the lake. He stared at the house until he saw Marge walk out on the side deck.

"Did you see Carson on your way in?" Marge asked.

Jack shook his head and walked to the house. Marge's face was severely drawn and her eyes were dull in a way that Jack had never before seen. She held out both hands to him and grabbed his so tightly that he almost cried out.

"I haven't the slightest idea what to do or say, Marge."

"Don't try, Jack. I've cried till the tears ran dry and thought till my mind's a blank. Just come and sit with me for a while."

They sat and looked at the river for a long time. As he waited for her to speak, Jack felt the sadness in the house gather around him palpably. When she finally broke the silence, her voice seemed cool and distant.

"You probably shouldn't be around for a while. There are going to be a lot of police, a lot of questions. There's nothing you can really do, anyway."

"How long were they here?"

"They showed up just after I spoke with you at noon. They were here when I talked with you at 3:00, but you know that. They finished the search about 5:00.

Didn't find anything. A guy from the Georgia Bureau of Investigation stayed and questioned me for another hour. I told him I didn't know anything about anything."

"What were they looking for? I mean, what did the search warrant say?"

"Marijuana. They seemed to think that Smiley had already harvested some of the plant before . . ."

"Had he, Marge?"

"No. Well, just a few plants that he brought in about a week ago. They didn't find that though. That's still up in the stash with the money."

"Maybe I better get that shit out of here, Marge. Now."

They walked upstairs to Marge and Smiley's bedroom, and Jack opened the door to the large walk-in closet. Marge stepped up on a small stool and pushed open a two-foot-square trap door in the back right-hand corner of the ceiling. She reached up and pulled out a waterproof canvas shoulder satchel, which she handed to Jack, and then an army issue ammunition can.

"The herb's in the ammo can," Marge said.

Jack opened the can and found six airtight, seal-a-meal packets of primo reefer.

"The money in that?" he asked, nodding to the satchel.

"A hundred thousand, I think. What's left of Smiley's Belize money."

"That's what he told me he had left. You need to get that out of here, too. Get it secured. They might come back anytime."

They walked out to the deck and stood for an awkward moment. When Jack slipped his arm around

Marge's waist she pulled away.

"Sorry, Jack. I don't know why I did that. Everything seems so turned around I just . . . "

As her words trailed off, Marge's gaze wandered to the treeline on the edge of the yard. Carson, her son, was striding toward them. He was decked out in full camouflage dress and wore a quiver of arrows on his back and a large hunting knife on his belt. In his right hand he carried a compound hunting bow. In his left hand he carried a large rabbit by the ears. His face was frozen in a mask of pain and anger and he did not acknowledge Jack or Marge as he passed them on the way to the game-cleaning table set between two oaks in the back yard.

Jack watched the boy sling the rabbit up on the table, pull his knife from its scabbard, and almost viciously rip the rabbit's belly open. When Jack turned back to Marge, he saw her watching the boy with tear-filled eyes.

"I've got to be strong for the kids, but I swear, Jack, I feel so empty inside that there doesn't seem to be anything in me to give."

"I know, Marge. This whole thing is so monstrous, so far beyond my understanding that . . . I'm gonna try to find out what happened. I need to know—need to get a grip on it before I can let it go."

Marge took his hands and held them once again very tightly. "Me too, Jack. I'm afraid. When I saw Smiley's picture on TV, I felt like I was losing my mind. I mean really losing my mind. Like some terrible vacuum was sucking it out of my head. I could literally feel it slipping away from me. It's not right to ask, but I don't feel like I have any choice. Find out who did this, Jack. And why. Maybe if I can make some goddamn sense of all this, I can keep my sanity."

"I'm gonna ride up to the ridge and try to think things through. Meanwhile, have you talked to a lawyer?"

"No. And I don't even know when they are going to release Smiley's body. They were going to perform an autopsy today. I haven't felt up to calling them yet."

"I'm going to see Yeats Murphy tomorrow and retain him for you. It may be a good idea for you to call him now. Fill him in on what you know. Tell him I'll be in town tomorrow. And, Marge, listen to anything he has to say. You can trust the man."

Jack got in his truck and looked back to the deck where Marge stood, arms wrapped tightly around her bosom. He feared that the sensitivity that made her so lovely might be her undoing as the weight of this experience bore down upon her.

* * *

A biting wind greeted Jack when he got out of the truck to open the gate across his driveway. The cold front moving through was the third in a series of wintry blasts that had penetrated the South much earlier than usual that autumn. Jack felt a rise in his spirits immediately after locking the gate behind him. Solitude. He had missed the ridge much more than he had realized. For a moment, all of the events of the past three weeks seemed illusory, dreamlike. But only for a moment.

Jack grabbed a few sticks of seasoned red oak from the woodpile and let himself in the unlocked front door of the cabin, noting with satisfaction that everything appeared to be in order. In all of his years on the ridge, he had never locked the door, never had a real intruder. Once, upon returning after a four-month summer absence, he had found a polite note from a hunter who, lost and thirsty, had let himself in for a drink of water.

Within fifteen minutes, the crackling fire in the oversized fireplace had chased the chill from the cabin. Jack sat down on the corduroy cushioned sofa in front of the fireplace and put his feet up on the unfinished oak coffee table. In the instant that he fully settled into the cushions, he knew that he was going to take a drink. He rolled the idea over in his mind and found it entirely appropriate and to his liking.

He rose and walked into the kitchen, opened a cabinet over the sink, and took down a wooden box engraved with a crest and the words *Glen Grant*. A friend in the oil business in Aberdeen, Scotland, had given him the Scotch shortly after his acquittal three years earlier with the admonition not to waste it on the palates of fools or the wrong occasion. At least the occasion is right, he thought.

When he lifted the small copper latch, the box opened into equal halves, with a cut glass decanter and a bottle of twenty-five-year-old Scotch nestled into indented yellow silk cushions. The label on the bottle indicated that the precious liquor was from the proprietor's reserve and was issued only every other year.

Jack filled a pint Ball jar with spring water from the tap and repaired with it, the bottle, and a shot glass to the sofa. He poured the dark whiskey into the glass and studied it for a long moment before reaching for it. Then he raised his glass to Smiley. Here's to you, brother, he thought as he drained the glass.

The single malt whiskey was extremely full-bodied with just a hint of smoke in the finish. Jack felt it hit his stomach and then fan upward in waves of warmth until his entire chest glowed. After three shots of Scotch, he remembered the herb in the truck and rose to retrieve it.

Back at the fireplace, Jack opened the ammo can and removed one of the six packets. He hefted it and estimated it to be a quarter pound. When he slit the bag, a deep, winy indica perfume wafted up, filling the room. He pulled out a manicured flower and noted its plump fullness and extreme density. He broke down enough of the herb for a large joint and found no seeds. A truly distinctive strain, he thought. I've never seen anything quite like it before. He searched his memory for the name Smiley had used—Oakland Indica.

After rummaging through the kitchen drawers, Jack found a pack of cabaret-width Club papers and rolled a fat number. As he lit the joint, the uniqueness of the taste and bouquet immediately impressed him. By the time he had finished half the joint, his ears were ringing and his heart was racing in his chest. Powerful shit.

Jack stared into the fire and lost himself. There is a monster out there and he's got your shit, Smiley, he thought. That's how I'm gonna find him, too, Smiley. Through the shit.

Jack drank another shot of Scotch and leaned back on the sofa. As he stared into the fire, a plan began to form.

CHAPTER 9

At 4:15 Sunday afternoon, Courtney Fowler typed the last word of her story and felt the fatigue that she had somehow managed to keep at bay wash over her. The three-hour nap the night before was the only sleep that she had had since early Friday morning. Between the interminable police interviews and the frantic rush to meet a five o'clock deadline, her last reserves of adrenaline and willpower had been exhausted.

She closed her eyes and gently massaged her temples. I need to get away from all of this for a while, she thought. And I don't want to be alone.

When Courtney opened her eyes and looked at the last page of her article, the symbols on the paper swam before her eyes. She assembled the six typewritten pages and took them down the hall to her proofreader for a final vetting.

On the way back to her office, Courtney decided to call Tom Doyle. She was relieved when he answered on the third ring.

"Do you have any comfort to give a very done-in lady?"

"At this moment, I am alone with Debussy and a bottle of Chateau Margeaux. Sound good?"

"Divine. Tom, this has been a rough time and I'm shaky inside and out and I—well, I guess I'm inviting myself over for the night. How do you feel about a house guest?"

"I feel very gratified that you chose to call me. You sound as weak as a kitten. Shall I pick you up?"

"No. I can make it just about that far. And Tom, this means a lot."

"That goes both ways, love. Hurry on."

Courtney replaced the receiver with a certain relief. This was the first time in many hours that she had a good feeling about what was coming up around the next bend. Stand up, she thought, collect your things, put on your coat and walk out of here, and don't tell anyone where you are going. Escape. Now!

Lois Poole, the only secretary on duty that day, stuck her head into the office just as Courtney was putting on her coat.

"You've got a call on line three, Ms. Fowler. I know that you said no calls, but this one is kind of strange. It's a man—sounds like he's whispering—said he had information about the Smiley murder and that he'd only talk to you."

Courtney decided not to take the call and started to walk out. Then, through the haze of her fatigue, she felt a prick of hesitation and returned to her desk. Goddamn all, she thought. This better be good.

"This is Courtney Fowler. Who is calling?"

"No names, Miss Fowler," a barely audible male voice whispered. "Reverend Clyde and Clint. They might be involved in that crucifixion that you reported on yesterday."

Courtney heard the line go dead before she could get a question out of her mouth, and she slammed the receiver violently. No more, she thought, I can't bear another goddamn thing. She quickly wrote the names

Reverend Clyde and Clint on her note pad. Then she fled her office and did not stop until she reached her car. She took deep breaths of the cold afternoon air and sped toward a safe port named Tom Doyle.

***

Doc Cole hung up his car phone and increased his speed from fifty-five to sixty-five miles per hour. He wondered if there was any way that his call could be traced and then rejected the idea. He had thought about calling Courtney Fowler shortly after seeing her news report on the crucified man in the marijuana field. In a fit of nervousness, he had turned on the tube after Lucius O'Dell's visit early Saturday afternoon. He knew immediately that there was some connection between Lucius's rambling discourse and the horrible thing that he had seen on the screen. He had thought better of making the call, quickly packed an overnight bag, and driven up Highway 400 to Dahlonega, in the mountains. The mountains were jammed with weekend leaf watchers from the city and he had had a terrible time finding accommodations. He had finally found an overpriced room with a worn-out bed and no TV in a dumpy little motel five miles north of town. Thoughts of Lucius and the atrocity that Cole had seen on the tube had worried his waking hours and eventually pursued him in troubled sleep. He had awakened at dawn from a nightmare in which he was the man on the cross.

After breakfast on Sunday morning, Doc Cole had driven up to Brasstown Bald and taken in the magnificent view from the tallest mountain in Georgia. Upon making out the Atlanta skyline some ninety miles away, Doc reflected that this might be a good time for a real vacation. Somewhere south. The Yucatán or maybe Jamaica. This idea had been powerfully reinforced when, at 4:30 P.M., a news broadcast had related that Lucius O'Dell, age forty-four, had been found murdered in his home Sunday afternoon. O'Dell was found by a co-worker concerned by Lucius's several-day absence from work. According to the announcer, Lucius had been tied to a chair, shot between the eyes, and relieved of his ears with a sharp instrument. He had received numerous burns on his chest. When the newscast ended, Doc had reached for the phone.

No more publicity, Doc thought, as he drove resolutely toward his home. God only knows how many scripts they found at Lucius's house. They'll want to question me. It will be all over the media. Sex Crazed Shrink Linked to Ear Chop Murders. I'm outta here, he thought. I'll drop by the house and pack. Drive to Jacksonville. Fly south from there. Please don't let them be waiting when I get home.

CHAPTER 10

Jack Lee bolted from bed when the alarm clock sounded at 5:00 Monday morning. He staggered toward the kitchen in the dark and fumbled about unsuccessfully for the clock. By the time he remembered the lights, the old wind-up had ground to a stop. It took several seconds for Jack to remember the reason for the presence of the furry creature in his mouth and the dull ache at the base of his skull. He stood and allowed himself to become reacquainted with all the old pains in all of the old familiar places. "Nice to see you again," he muttered to the hangover.

After showering, Jack brewed a pot of strong Ceylon tea and repaired to the fireplace. He added two sticks of seasoned oak to the banked coals and, after poking them, watched with satisfaction as the oak caught. By the time he had finished the second cup of tea, he felt warmed inside and out. Then he walked out the front door with the ammo can tucked under his arm, ready for the long day ahead.

The first rays of the rising sun were just beginning to play upon the gold dome of the capitol when Jack exited off I-20 onto Spring Street. Atlanta, capital of the New South, Jack thought wryly. He knew that the much-ballyhooed image of the New South was just that—image. And the image was equal in substance to a thin veneer of cheap Japanese shellac, beneath which lay the age-old mosaic of bigotry and racial animosity.

Integration had bred a new mutual contempt born of familiarity, personalized in a way never possible in the arm's-length days of segregation.

As Jack drove onto Spring Street, the street people, freshly risen from the slim comforts of cardboard mattresses, began the ghastly morning promenade in hopes that movement would bring warmth to their chilled bones. Jack shuddered and felt the urge to flee the city, forget everything that had happened, and retreat to the security of the ridge. Then, a flash of Smiley hanging on the cross chased all doubt from his mind.

Jack was greeted by a wide-eyed parking valet when he pulled the pickup into the underground lot at the Omni. "Man, we don't be parkin' no din-o-saurs down here," he said, laughing, as he handed Jack his ticket.

Just don't be messin' with what's under the seat, Jack thought as he walked up to ground level. He covered the short distance to Yeats Murphy's office on Nassau quickly, hoping that his hunch would be correct. Since his wife's death five years ago, Yeats had taken to spending half of his nights in a small suite of rooms that he had installed on the top floor of the two-storied building that housed his law practice. If he had not spent Sunday night there, Jack would have to spend an hour killing time in the inner-city, a thought that held no appeal.

When he reached the front door of the building, Jack reached down and pushed a small button hidden behind the molding at the bottom left-hand corner of the door. After a few seconds, he heard the static sound of an open intercom.

"And who might this be calling at such an indecent hour of the mornin'?" asked Yeats Murphy in a lilting voice filled with the Old South accent associated with the alleged upper class.

"It's Jack Lee, Yeats."

"Ah, Jackson Robert E. Lee, arch scoundrel and disturber of the mornin' peace. Hold on, I'll be right down."

Jack blanched at the sound of his full name. He had forgiven his parents for his name only after their deaths. Not that he was ashamed of the name. He had just come to hate the attention and comments that the usage of his full name had brought all through school and then, later, during his trial when the national press had keyed in on it and begun to portray him as some kind of modern-day Rhett Butler. Yeats Murphy was one of the only people in the world that he allowed the use of that name. He loved the old man dearly.

Jack watched the old man descend the staircase with an alacrity befitting a man twenty-five years his junior. Rather damn spry for sixty-nine, he thought.

Yeats Murphy was a six-foot, white-haired bloom of a man with twinkly blue eyes and bushy black eyebrows that dominated a long, handsome face amazingly free of wrinkles. He radiated tremendous energy, charm, and a joie de vivre so intense that uninformed adversaries tended to mistake him for a less than serious man, a fatal error. This morning he was dressed in white silk pajamas over which he wore a navy blue silk brocade robe that hung to the tops of his black, kid leather slippers. In his left hand, he held a Sobranie Balkan cigarette, the first of his daily ration of ten.

Yeats opened the door with his left hand and ushered Jack inside with a flowing, waist-high flourish of his right.

"Three years and nary a word, lad. Yet, I admit a certain rise in spirit when poor Marge told me that you would be favoring me with a visit. Come in and be welcome."

Jack walked in and stood before the man to whom he owed his freedom and felt a surge of affection. After a moment of mutual appraisal, they embraced in a manner not unlike that of a long-separated father and son.

"You said that you would be out of touch for a while. I never expected that it would be three years."

"I know that it's been too long, Yeats. If you have a few minutes, I'll explain."

"My schedule is clear until noon. Come up and we will talk over breakfast. After that, you can tell me about the trouble that has brought you to my door."

Jack found that the apartment fit precisely the memory of his last visit. The small living room was paneled in rosewood and furnished with a matching light brown leather sofa and easy chair. The gleaming oak floor was set off by an eight-foot-square maroon Persian rug. The room had the feel of a man's private quarters and Jack knew that Yeats entertained very few people in what was, essentially, his retreat.

Yeats made coffee for himself and tea for Jack in the combination kitchen and dining area where they talked while Yeats prepared breakfast. Jack told Yeats about his experiences on the ridge, wondering, as he did so, what his old friend's response would be. Yeats listened quietly, without interruption, until Jack had run out of words.

"And what is the most important thing that you learned during this time, Jack?"

"I learned how to be alone. To live with myself."

Yeats brought in platters served with large portions of cheddar and mushroom omelette, sliced tomato, whole wheat toast, and sliced honeydew melon. He sat and looked fondly at Jack, a soft smile on his face.

"That's a thing most people never get around to in this life. I can see that it has changed you. To tell the truth, I didn't think you had it in you. The ability to change, I mean. You learn a lot about people in the course of a trial, especially a messy one like yours. I admired you for the way you handled yourself, the way you stood by your people. I admired your intelligence and your heart and your loyalty, but I didn't think those qualities would save you from your stubbornness. I even wondered if acquittal might not be the worst thing for you. I feared you would jump right back into the game, keep burnin' the candle at both ends until there was nothin' left to burn. You wouldn't have lasted much longer, lad. I could see the edge of the shadow upon you. So, it does my old heart good to see you like this. Hell, listen to me. Long in the tooth, long in the wind, eh? Dig in before it gets cold."

They ate in silence, neither man wanting to finish the meal and get down to the business that sat uneasily between them. Jack finished first and waited for Yeats to break the silence. When Yeats had finished his food, he carefully placed his utensils on his plate and looked up at Jack. There was no twinkle in his eye.

"So you're anxious to be gettin' down to business, are you, lad?"

"There is a certain element of time involved."

"Before we step into my office and I go to playin' the lawyer, there is something that I want to put to you as a friend. It will require an open mind and your complete attention."

"Ready on both counts, Yeats."

Yeats excused himself and left the room. When he returned, he held a manilla folder. Jack saw his name written in red ink on the outside of the folder.

"When Marge called yesterday, I had occasion to poke around a bit in my files. I came upon your background report and spent some time with it last night. While I was reading it, an idea came to me that I would like to share with you. Now, when you left the university in your senior year, you were carrying a 3.8 average out of a possible 4 points."

"I didn't leave the university, Yeats. I was expelled permanently."

Jack felt anger that he thought had long since died. He had gone to the university on a full scholarship. A high school all-American end, great things had been predicted for him and much had been expected.

In his second week of practice, Jack had caught a short pass on a dinky down-and-out pattern and run seventy-five yards for a touchdown. During the course of the run, the absurdity of what he was doing had come to him with startling clarity. When he reached the goal line, Jack dropped the ball and without breaking stride ran directly to the dressing room. The incredulous receiver coach pursued him and asked him what he thought he was doing. "I quit," was the only explanation that he gave the coach. Many people never forgave Jack that transgression.

Later, in his senior year, Jack had joined the protest against Nixon's invasion of Cambodia. A group of "outside agitators" had shown up during the demonstration wearing khaki clothes and espousing a violent, confrontational approach. The university administration, trembling with fear, had called in a contingent of riot police. When a non-violent stand-off occurred, one of the outsiders had emerged with a tear gas container. "If they won't gas us, we'll gas ourselves," the brown shirt had said as he began to open the cannister. "Maybe that'll get these grit-eating rednecks off their asses."

Jack had taken the cannister from the non-student, who turned out to be an SDS organizer from Washington, D.C. In the process, he had broken the man's right kneecap and his left arm. This action had been caught on film and although a serious riot had been averted, Jack had been expelled from school with no possibility of reinstatement. Jack had left with a feeling that the severity of his punishment had been linked to his failure to perform on the football field.

"Are you there, lad?"

"Sorry, Yeats. Go ahead."

"No criminal charges were ever filed in the incident that lead to your expulsion, correct?"

"Correct. The fella seemed to be in a big hurry to get out of town."

"A lot of things change in twenty years, Jack. There's an entirely new administration at the university now. Some good friends of mine have gained prominence in the law school. New exemption tests have been introduced to expedite the completion of undergraduate requirements for people like you. With a little help, I think that we could get your B.A. and your law degree in four years."

Jack started to protest but Yeats cut him off with the thrust of an open palm toward him. "You agreed to listen. Hear me out. I never spoke much to you about my son. Ritchie would have been forty-five this year, just like you. He was in his second year of law school when he was killed in the wreck. A miserable drunk crossed over the center line and hit him head on. Some sons don't want to follow in their father's footsteps. Ritchie did. Murphy and Murphy. We had it all planned, Jack. He was brilliant, first in his class. A jewel of a boy who can never be replaced. I'd never want to try to replace him. But, I've built something here. One of the most prestigious criminal practices in the country. And there is no one after me to carry it on. You are made for it. During your trial you showed me that you have the instincts for criminal law. You can't learn that in school. Oh sure, you can pick up a few things in school, but, mainly, school is a formality. I'll teach you what you really need to know. I'll guide you every step of the way. Introduce you to the people you need to know. When you are ready, I'll step aside and turn the whole damn thing over to you. You tell me that you've found a woman that you care about. That you don't know about your future. Take this future, Jack. A man with a mind like yours needs a career. What do you say, lad?"

Jack was deeply moved by the old man's words. He knew that Yeats had offered him everything he had to give. That he had essentially offered Jack the most precious thing of all—himself. He also knew immediately that he would not accept the offer, that his path lay in another direction. He sat quietly for a long moment, seeking the right words.

"Yeats, that is the kindest, the most generous offer that has ever been made to me. I love you for making it and I hope that you will accept my answer with the love and the thanks intended. I can't accept. It's true that I don't know what the future holds. I do know that I'll never live in this world in a regular way. At this moment, that is the only thing that I am sure of. I'm sorry."

A look of hurt passed over Yeats's face as he listened to Jack. Then, a smile, wise and knowing, appeared and almost covered the hurt.

"The offer remains open, lad. Now, shall we step into my office?"

At the door to Yeats's office, just across the hall from his apartment, Yeats turned and faced Jack.

"I was truly sorry to hear about Smiley. I purposefully did not bring up the subject earlier so that we could have a little time together free of grief.

Jack felt the air change when they entered the office. Yeats walked behind his desk and motioned Jack to the straight-backed chair in front of it. After lighting a cigarette, Yeats leaned back and blew a long plume of smoke toward the ceiling. Then, in a single, fluid motion, he leaned forward and fixed Jack with a steady gaze. His face had a predatory look of concentration and his body was motionless.

"What's on your mind, Jack?"

Jack was mildly awed by the change in Yeats in spite of his familiarity with the cold, merciless aspect that Yeats assumed when he entered the office. He could feel the steel in the man behind the desk.

"How do things look for Marge, Yeats? Does she have anything to worry about legally?"

"Legally, Marge is going to be fine. I'm going to see to that. Emotionally, well, that's another thing."

"I'll take care of the fees. Just let me know."

"You can't afford my fees anymore, lad. Besides, this is off the books. Now, spit it out Jack. What's on your mind?"

"I need to hire an investigator. A good one. Someone who's well connected with the boys down-town and willing to work on the Q.T. Completely off the record. Sound like anyone you know?"

"What the fuck do you need with an investigator, Jack?"

"As an officer of the court, you don't want to know."

Yeats fell back into his chair and threw his hands up into the air, dropping an ash on his left shoulder in the process. He brushed the ash from his robe angrily and stood.

"So, you want to find Smiley's murderer? Is that it? Then what? An eye for an eye? Revenge? You can't afford to get mixed up in this. You are not an average citizen, Jack. If they ever get another clear shot at you, they'll bury you. Figuratively or literally. You skated last time and they hate you for it. Stay away from this! We're deal-ing with a serial killer here. They've called out all the dogs on this one."

"Wait a minute, Yeats. What do you mean serial killer?"

"When's the last time you heard the news?"

"I saw yesterday's paper just before I went up to the ridge."

"Holy shit, lad. Two more have lost their ears since then."

Jack felt his bowels loosen.

"Crucified?"

"No. Shot between the eyes. Burns on their upper bodies. Ears cut off. Both men were found in their homes. Tied to chairs. These guys were tortured. And listen to this. The first guy was found yesterday afternoon. One Lucius O'Dell. A helicopter pilot, Jack. Employed by the State of Georgia. He was in the Marijuana Eradication Program. Guess where he was flying last week?"

"Carroll County."

"You're fast lad. The second victim was Dr. Benjamin Cole, psychiatrist. Doc Cole, the writing doctor. Script writer extraordinaire. Guess who was on his client list?"

"Lucius O'Dell?"

"None other."

"You think the same person that did Smiley did these other guys, too?"

"Well, look at it this way. Three bodies in thirty-six hours. The factor of the ears. Timewise, this doesn't follow the pattern of copycat killings. Too close together. Then, Smiley is found in a Carroll County pot field, O'Dell can be placed in the approximate area at roughly the same time in a legal capacity related to pot, and the good doctor is involved with O'Dell in a doctor-client relationship. Too many connections to be coincidence, wouldn't you think?"

"I don't know what to think, Yeats. My head's spinning."

"You are not alone in that, lad. This is national news. It was the lead story on all the networks last evening. That was on the basis of Smiley and O'Dell. It's only intensified since they found Doc Cole. He was involved in a high-profile sex scandal a few years back. The press is having a field day with that. The governor has already called for an FBI task force. Now, do you see why I say that you need to stay out of it? Jackson Robert E. Lee, Rhett Butler incarnate. Remember New Orleans? If the paparazzi link you to this, they will have an absolute feeding frenzy. You're old news, Jack. Leave it that way. Walk away. There is nothing for you in this situation."

"I still need an investigator."

"Goddamnit, haven't you listened to a word I've said? Back off!"

"I listened, Yeats. I still need a name. I thought you would be the best person to ask. Thanks for breakfast," Jack said as he rose from his chair.

"Oh, sit down you stubborn bastard. I can see that your mule blood's up. If I can't talk you out of this, I may as well make sure that you don't end up with some shyster."

Yeats pulled a business card from his desk drawer and picked up the phone.

"You free all day?" he asked Jack as he dialed.

"Anytime after 1:00."

After a brief conversation, Yeats hung up the phone, leaned forward, and handed Jack a business card. The name in the middle of the card was Darrell Day. At the bottom left of the card, the word *Investigations* was printed. At the bottom right, a Buckhead address on Peachtree and a telephone number.

"Darrell said to meet him at Manuel's Tavern at 1:00. He has a working lunch at 12:00 in mid-town and an appointment on the south side shortly after 2:00. He said to tell you that he can only give you thirty minutes on such short notice."

"What's the skinny on this guy, Yeats?"

"Retired from the Bureau five years ago under pressure. He was Agent-in-Charge of the Atlanta office. Refused to go along with a cover-up of improprieties committed during the course of a Justice Department bribery investigation of city officials. Got shipped to some podunk assignment in Wyoming as punishment. Finished out his thirty years there, then retired. Came back here and hung out a shingle. The guy's straight up, Jack. His word is good. Good contacts. Brilliant and lucky. Nobody in ten states can touch him."

"That's high praise coming from you."

"Not as high as the bill you will receive if he decides to take you on."

"How will I recognize him?"

"About six feet. Strong build. Dark hair. Heavy, three-shave-a-day beard. Said he's wearing a blue blazer and a red tie. Coal black eyes that look like they can kill you. You can't miss those eyes."

"Thanks, Yeats."

"You are not welcome. If you need me, call. If not, let me know when it's over."

Jack collected the truck and checked the contents of the ammo can under the seat. The cab immediately filled with the perfume of the herb. If anyone can help me, it's the Thin Man, he thought.

Traffic was light as he took Spring down to Peachtree and took a left. He thought about Deborah and felt a twinge of regret. He was torn about what to tell her, if anything. I'll see her this afternoon when she gets home from work, he thought. Try to explain things. Can't deal with that now.

Jack cleared his mind and focused on the best way to present his proposition to the Thin Man. By the time he turned left on West Paces Ferry Road, he had decided that a straightforward presentation of the facts was best. He was looking forward to seeing Thin and Lucy. They were one of the longest-married couples that he knew among his age group. Almost twenty years, he thought.

West Paces Ferry was the prestige row of Atlanta. Living there was a sign of having arrived. The extravagant homes and mini-estates stood resplendent among the hardwoods that carefully dotted the immaculate grounds filled with ornamental flowers and shrubs. As he passed the governor's mansion, Jack wondered if any of the neighbors had any idea of the nature of the new tenants who had crashed the block just a few years earlier.

When he saw the nine-foot-tall black cast-iron fence, Jack slowed down and turned left onto the driveway of a three-story, neo-Victorian mansion. The red brick monster was set back three hundred feet from the road in the middle of four acres. Jack got out of the truck and walked up to the locked gate. Beside a small

black, cast-iron bench with a canopy stood a five-foot
iron pole with a speaker attached to the top. Jack
pushed the button just under the speaker. After a few
seconds, the unmistakable high-pitched voice of Lucy
floated through the speaker.

"Who's calling, please."

"It's Jack Lee, Lucy."

"Well heavens to Betsy, Jack. What a surprise. Let
me open the gate for you."

Jack heard the hum of an electric motor and the
gate opened briskly inward. He drove around to the
back of the mansion and parked in a space marked
Domestic Help. As he got out of the truck, he heard a
door open and turned to see Lucy coming down the
back steps in a flowing white caftan.

"Oh, Jack, you were always such a joker." Lucy
said, walking toward him with arms extended.

Jack felt himself being crushed in the mauling
embrace of Anton Ledbetter, aka Lucy, and once known
on the street as Lucifer. He had acquired that sobriquet
during a melee with five bikers who had broken into
Thin's house in 1970 with the intention of ripping off the
fabled "King of the Strip." Upon hearing the soprano
suggestion that, if they left immediately, no one would
be hurt, the drunken bikers had burst into gales of
laughter. That had deeply offended the capable but normally non-violent Anton.

When an ambulance attendant had been overheard
asking one of the broken bikers what happened to him,
people on the sidewalk in front of Thin's house heard
him mutter, "Ran into Lucifer, man." Within minutes, the
Strip, an area roughly between Tenth and Fourteenth

streets on Peachtree that housed Atlanta's open-air counterculture circus, was awash with tales of Lucifer and the bikers. On the street the next day, Anton had been hailed with cries of "Lucifer! Lucifer!" A minor legend had been born.

Jack broke free from the grasp of the blond giant and viewed him with amazement made more grand through absence. Lucy was six seven and possessed the blue-eyed chiseled visage of a Norse god. His fire hydrant of a neck sat upon yard-wide shoulders below which a massive, fifty-two inch chest tapered radically to a thirty-one inch waist.

"Nice to see you, too, Lucy. Is the Thin Man around?"

"Indeed he is and I know that he will be just thrilled to see you. Please come in, Jack."

Jack was led into the vast room that occupied the entire first floor. The room was lit solely by three stained glass windows that ran from the polished black marble floors to the fifteen-foot ceiling. The windows admitted a slowly-changing kaleidoscope of colors that ranged from muted purple to dazzling gold, cerulean blue to ruby red, with hypnotic effect. At either end of the room, huge fireplaces held fires that were strangely void of brightness and that did little to dispel the vague chill that hung in the air. The only furniture was a long wooden table with twelve highbacked, crimson-cushioned chairs. The overall effect was medieval and produced an elusive, atavistic stirring in Jack.

When Lucy excused himself and disappeared up the mahogany staircase in search of Thin, Jack moved to the fireplace at the south end of the room. As the fire chased the chill from his bones, he reflected on the man who dwelled in this bizarre abode. Thin was a high school drop-out who had made his first fortune in psychedelics, primarily LSD, in the glory days of the late sixties. During those days, Atlanta was the distribution capital of the South, although it was not unusual for buyers to appear from as far away as Michigan and Arizona. Combining high native intelligence with a natural feel for capitalism and an almost uncanny judgment of human character, the Thin Man had risen rapidly and never taken a fall. Rumor held that the Thin Man was the keeper of certain secrets concerning several people in high places in return for noninterference in his life. Jack neither knew nor cared. He knew Thin to be scrupulously honest and fastidiously discreet. He also knew that Thin eschewed the use or sale of narcotics. When psychedelics went out of fashion, Thin had turned to high quality marijuana and had become the primary broker in Atlanta for the growing domestic herb market. Jack had reason to believe that Thin would have knowledge of any exotic herb transactions involving fifty pounds or more.

"Jack Lee."

The deeply-voiced sound of his name drifted down to Jack from the top of the staircase. He looked up to see the black-clad Thin Man standing at the head of the stairs, a sober look upon his narrow, angular face. The rail-thin body descended the stairs in an elegant dance of angles.

Jack's attention was called at once to the man's eyes. They were light brown with a yellowish cast. Cat eyes. The face wherein those eyes resided was long, severely lean, almost cadaverous. The close-cropped skullcap of iron-gray hair added to the suggestion of asceticism. The reedy body might have carried 130 pounds on its five-foot ten-inch frame.

Jack felt the Thin Man's eyes probing him as he walked from the bottom of the stairs to the fireplace where Jack stood. The faraway gaze of the Thin Man was to the psychedelic warrior what the thousand-yard stare was to war-weary combat veterans. At times, his eyes gave the impression that they were fixed on objects in far-flung galaxies.

"It's good to see you after all these years, Jack," said the Thin Man, offering his long-fingered, bony hand.

Jack shook the offered hand, which was warm and surprisingly strong.

"The pleasure is mutual, Thin. I wish the occasion were a happier one."

"I suspected that this was not a social call. This is about Smiley and the others."

"Not the others, just Smiley."

"Shall we stroll while we talk?"

Jack nodded and began to walk toward the door.

"No, Jack. We'll walk in here. Come."

Jack fell into a slow-paced walk beside Thin, noticing as he did so a barely discernible path worn into the black marble. The path ran the length of the long floor and rounded off the corner at the end of the room.

"What do you think of the room, Jack?"

"It's both beautiful and unsettling. I had a sensation of time slipping backwards when I first entered."

"I know the feeling. I saw this room in a dream. The dream was very vivid, and I awoke with the feeling that I was supposed to recreate the dreamroom in the waking world. At first, I resisted. Then, the resistance brought on a restlessness that left me feeling distracted and vaguely unsatisfied. Finally, I knocked out all of the walls down here and created this. At the moment of completion, I was filled with a surpassing feeling of peace. Now I spend hours at a time walking this room. My mind empties. It becomes a form of walking meditation. I have been meditating on evil since I saw those pictures of Smiley. What are your thoughts on evil, Jack?"

They walked in silence for some time. Jack was aware of the feeling that he had somehow stepped across a threshold into another time and place.

"I believe in the existence of evil. I think that the exercise of evil by human beings requires an unusual degree of intelligence and volition. But, there is a different kind of evil altogether. Something elemental. Perfect in itself. Its own cause and effect. I really don't have the words to express what I mean."

"That is very interesting, Jack. I have a feel for the distinction that you are trying to make. I think that Smiley crossed the path of something, someone evil. Something beyond simple madness."

"I intend to find out, Thin. I've come to ask for your help."

"I sensed that. What do you have in mind?"

"Before Smiley was killed, he approached me about selling his crop for him. He had five hundred plants and was expecting two hundred and fifty pounds. I've been out of the Trade for over three years, but I agreed, reluctantly, because I had a bad feeling about

Smiley trying to get off the shit by himself. The police reports mentioned only two hundred plants. I think whoever did Smiley also made off with over half the crop. I've got a pound of herb with me. Some bud that he brought in early. It's very distinctive, Thin. I was hoping that you would take a look at it and let me know if you happen to see a good-sized load of this herb on the block. I think somebody out there has a hundred and a quarter—maybe a hundred and a half drying as we speak. Cleaning that much shit takes a lot of time. Maybe someone will try to dump it all rough. I don't know, Thin. It's the only angle I've got to work on. If anyone is in a better position than you to get a shot at seeing something that size, I don't know them."

"Where is the herb, Jack?"

"In the truck."

"Why don't you bring it in and let me take a look."

Jack returned to the room to find Thin sitting at the head of the long table. In front of him was a rolling tray and a pack of Bambu papers. He motioned Jack to the chair on his right.

Jack placed the ammo can on the table and sat down. When he opened the can, the perfume of the herb immediately saturated the air around them. Thin's eyes lit up as he sniffed the air.

"That is a rather distinctive bouquet," Thin said.

"Please, help yourself," Jack said as he handed one of the unopened packets to Thin.

Thin produced a small penknife and slit the packet. Then he poured the contents onto the tray, selected a plump bud, and gently squeezed it under his nose.

"This is the first time that I have seen this on the

East Coast," Thin said.

"You know the strain?"

"Offhand, I would guess Oakland Indica. Of course, I would need to smoke it to be sure," he said with a smile. "May I?"

"Please."

Jack watched as Thin carefully broke the flower down into tiny pieces with his long fingers. A beam of yellow-gold light fell across the tray, illuminating the silvery crystals of resin that coated the herb.

After rolling the joint, Thin took several long draws before lighting up.

"Incredible taste, is it not? Like fine, aged Port."

Jack nodded in assent and watched Thin light the joint, inhale deeply, and, after holding the smoke in his lungs for five seconds, exhale a dense cloud that filled the air with a deep, pungent aroma. When he offered the joint to Jack, Jack held up his hand and shook his head. Thin took one more large toke and put the joint on the tray. Blue-gray smoke curled upward from it. Various colored beams of light from the stained glass windows played upon the smoke as it rose.

Thin closed his eyes and sat back in his chair. A minute or so later, when he opened them, his eyes were somewhat red and glassy. The sharp features of his face had softened noticeably.

"Definitely Oakland Indica. Developed by the Dutch boys in a selective breeding program. Sold at the rate of three dollars per seed by mail order catalog."

"Then you think that you could recognize this specific crop if you saw it?"

"Most likely."

"Then what do you say, Thin? Will you help me?"

"Help you do what, Jack? What do you get from this? What happens to the monster that did this to Smiley?"

"I haven't thought that far along, yet."

"You are kidding one of us, but I don't think it's me. You know, the act of revenge often consumes all parties involved. I would hate to think that, in the process of helping you, I was contributing to your own demise."

"Thin, you're a deep bastard for a high school drop-out."

Thin smiled, exposing his upper row of tiny, flawless, pearl-like teeth. Then he threw back his head and laughed a deep laugh that rolled and echoed throughout the cavernous room. It was the kind of laugh that causes small children to break into tears and large dogs to turn tail and run. Jack felt a chill as he listened to it.

"Deep doesn't even come close, Jack. Leave this herb with me. How can I contact you if I need to?"

"I'm going to be on the move. How about me checking in with you by phone once a day?"

Thin removed a small note pad from his shirt pocket and wrote a number down. He ripped the page out and handed it to Jack.

"That is a very private line. Call in the mornings between eight and nine. Pay phone only. Wait a couple of days before calling."

"Thanks, Thin. I'll be in touch."

"No thanks necessary. Smiley was one of the good guys. This feels rather personal to me, too. Be careful out there."

CHAPTER 11

Courtney Fowler was awakened by the pleasant aroma of freshly brewed coffee. She stretched luxuriously and lay back in the warm bed with her eyes closed.

As she began to return to full consciousness, the awareness that she was not in her own bed produced a feeling of disorientation. She could not remember how she came to be in this strange bed. When she opened her eyes and saw her clothes folded neatly on a chair in the corner, she experienced a momentary panic. Finally, when she realized that she was at Tom's, she relaxed.

Courtney called out Tom's name and waited, trying to reconstruct the events of the past evening. Her mind was a total blank. When Tom opened the door and walked to the bed carrying a tray of coffee, orange juice, and bagels with cream cheese, she felt blood rush to her cheeks.

"Tom, I don't remember . . . anything. The last thing I remember is parking the car downstairs. What happened?"

"I bored you to sleep in less than ten minutes," Tom said, smiling.

"Oh, God. I'm sorry, Tom."

"Don't be, you were great."

Courtney suddenly became aware of her nakedness beneath the covers.

"Did we . . . ? Did you . . . ?"

"I had my way with you. Don't you remember anything?" Tom asked as he settled the tray across her lap.

"Oh, no, I'm so embarrassed. Please tell me what happened."

"Well, my dear, you drank half a glass of wine and fell asleep in mid-sentence. I carried you back here, disrobed you, and tucked you in. You have slept for approximately fifteen and one-half hours."

"What time is it?"

"A little after 9:00."

"Damn, I'm late."

Courtney removed the tray that straddled her waist and placed it beside her on the bed. Gently, but firmly, Tom pushed her back into the pillows and replaced the tray.

"You're not going anywhere until you have breakfast. You may be a girl wonder, but even you must sleep and take nourishment occasionally."

"Have you heard the news recently?"

"Of course I've heard the news lately. I'm a newsman, remember? Now, I'm going to leave you with your breakfast. When you finish, get dressed and come join me. I will fill you in then."

Courtney found Tom staring out the picture window of his living room. She joined him at the window and saw that it was another beautiful day. Below them, Roswell Road was relatively free of traffic. When Tom turned to her, Courtney knew from the troubled look on his face that all was not well. He took her by the hand and led her to the sofa, where he gave her a clear, concise recap of events that had occurred while she had slept.

Courtney listened in amazed silence. It was some time after Tom had finished speaking before she was able to muster the words for the questions that she had.

"Dr. Benjamin Cole. THE Doc Cole of recent notoriety? And this O'Dell person was his patient?"

Tom nodded and remained silent.

"And O'Dell flew for the state? He was in Carroll County the week of the Smiley murder?"

"That's all I know and it's enough to make me very concerned for your safety. Whoever left that note on your door Friday night is still out there, Courtney. I don't know what the connection is in these murders, but there is a connection and you are somehow square in the middle of the picture. Do you know anything that sheds light on all of this? Are you sitting on anything?"

Courtney considered telling Tom about the call that she had received just before coming to his apartment then, in deference to a well-cultivated habit of secrecy regarding her work, rejected the idea.

"Why do you ask that?"

"I'm not sure. Just worried, I guess, that you might know something that this maniac would rather you didn't. Whatever, I think you should move in with me until this thing is resolved. I can't bear the idea of you being alone at night with this murderer out there. As a matter of fact, I insist. You already owe me two rainchecks and I'm calling in your markers. You really can't refuse."

Courtney admitted to herself that she felt a little frightened. More than a little, really. At the very least, this was an opportunity to spend some intimate time with Tom, an idea that gave her a pleasant tingling sensation in her lower belly.

"I accept. But only out of honor. No one's ever

accused me of welshing on an offer. I'm a healthy, rested female animal, buddy, so you better eat some vitamins."

Tom laughed and kissed her lightly. She pulled him back to her and kissed him long and deep. He took her hand and slipped a key into it.

"I go in at 4:00 and get off after the 11:00 news. I expect to find you lounging in next to nothing when I return. Seriously, let yourself in and make yourself at home."

"You're on. I'll do a shop after work and prepare us a midnight supper. Gotta run now."

When Courtney Fowler walked into her mid-town office at 10:30 Monday morning, she was greeted by the flashing red message light on her telephone and a stack of messages on her desk. She punched in Lois Poole's number and waited. When the secretary answered, Courtney could tell from the tone of her voice that something was up.

"Honey, all hell is breaking loose around here this morning. Have you heard about these two new murders?"

"I've heard, Lois, and I want you to round up everything that's gone into print about them since yesterday afternoon. And, Lois, are these messages on my desk up to date?"

"All except for Mr. Special Agent Tommy Dalton from the GBI. He's called back twice since 9:30. He said to tell you that he's going to stop by at 1:00 and to tell you that it is urgent that he speaks with you."

"OK, Lois, thanks."

Goddamn cops, she thought. They are going to put

me through the ringer again. I just don't have time for this shit. I told them I'd call if anything new came up.

She lifted her messages from the top of her notepad and saw the names *Reverend Clyde* and *Clint* scrawled upon the top page. She pondered the names for a moment before tearing the page out, carefully folding it, and placing it in a back corner of her desk drawer. I'll deal with that later, she thought. First things first.

She returned a call from her station manager and found out that he had sold her exclusive video footage of the Smiley murder scene to the networks for a very tidy sum. She accepted his long-winded praise impatiently and promised to devote her Saturday program exclusively to the murders.

Next, she called her publisher and received more praise, this time for the column that had just hit the streets in today's edition of *Atlanta Today*. Yes, she assured him, she would have a dynamite column ready for Friday's edition. No, she hadn't heard about the offers that were pouring in from newspapers around the country to publish her columns about the murders.

As soon as Courtney had dealt with all of her messages, she began to flog her Rolodex for names and numbers that might furnish some piece of information or a clue regarding the murders. After two hours on the phone, all she had to show for her efforts was a bad case of telephone ear.

Lois brought her a stack of newspapers and a cup of coffee. After reading the papers, she knew nothing more than when she began. She was becoming convinced, however, that the police had absolutely nothing to go on. Not a clue, she thought.

Courtney looked up at the wall clock and saw that it was five minutes past one. Time to call in a hired gun, she thought. She flipped through her Rolodex until she found Darrell Day's number. He had done some excellent work for her on the Japanese influence case. Maybe he could dig up something on this Reverend Clyde character. And Clint somebody. It was all she had to go on at the moment.

Darrell Day's secretary informed her that Mr. Day was out of the office but that she might reach him at Manuel's tavern before 1:30. Courtney was dialing the number to Manuel's when someone rapped smartly on her door.

She hung up the phone and rose to answer the door. Before she could reach it, a tall young man in a trenchcoat opened the door and walked in.

"Please come in," Courtney said a bit more sarcastically than she had intended.

"Sorry about that," the man said.

It was obvious to Courtney that the man was not in the least sorry for having barged into her office. On second glance, he was not as young as she had thought. Maybe early forties. He had brush-cut light blond hair, light blue eyes, and a cruel slit of a mouth that marred an otherwise handsome face. He carried himself cockily and made no effort to hide his frank, sexual appraisal of her. If you ordered a detective from a catalog, she thought, this is what you would get. She knew immediately that she would share nothing with this man.

"I'm Tommy Dalton, Miss Fowler. I'm with the GBI and we need to talk."

"Mr. Dalton, I can't add a thing to the statement

that I've already given to the police in Carroll County. Have you seen the statement?"

"I have, but we still need to ask you some questions. I was hoping we could keep this informal. Maybe talk over a bite of lunch. You can call me Tommy, by the way."

"Mr. Dalton, I'm extremely busy right now. I'm sure that you must be, too. There is really nothing that I can add to that statement. If you leave me a number, I'll call you if I remember anything or find out anything that I think you should know."

"Miss Fowler, we can do this my way, or the hard way. If you would rather come down to the Peter's building for formal questioning, that can be arranged. It's up to you."

Courtney read the hardness in the man's eyes and realized that he could make a real nuisance of himself if he chose to. Changing tacks, she gave him a sweet smile and held her palms up in a gesture of helplessness.

"I'm sorry. Tommy, you said? I've been under a lot of pressure lately and my blood sugar tends to drop when that happens. As a matter of fact, I could really use a bite of lunch. If the offer is still open, of course."

"The offer is definitely still open Miss . . . Courtney. May I call you Courtney?"

"By all means, Tommy. I need to make just one brief call before we go. Would you mind waiting in the front lobby? I'll just be a minute."

When Dalton closed the office door behind him, Courtney redialed the number for Manuel's and heard a bartender blare, "Hello, Manuel's" over the hubbub of the noisy lunchtime crowd. Yes, Darrell Day was there.

She removed the folded piece of paper from her drawer and waited.

CHAPTER 12

Jack Lee walked into the front door of Manuel's Tavern at 1:00. The place was doing a brisk lunch business and the air was filled with sounds of voices, tinkling glass, active cutlery, and smoke. At the bar to his right, Jack saw a tall dark-haired man wearing a blue blazer and a red tie. When Jack was three steps away, the man turned to the fellow on his right and gave Jack a clear view of his face, which contained a pair of moist, dark, spaniel eyes. Those puppy eyes definitely did not fit Yeats's description of Darrell Day.

Jack stopped and surveyed the room. In the last booth on the left, a man in a blue blazer sat alone, staring down at his coffee cup. When he raised his head and looked toward the door, he revealed a pair of menacing black eyes aglow in slightly sunken sockets. Jack approached the booth under the scrutiny of those baleful eyes.

"Mr. Day?"

"Have a seat, Mr. Lee."

Jack slid into the booth and studied the world-weary face of Darrell Day. Deep crow's feet extended from the corners of his eyes to the hairline at each temple. A pair of creases followed a strong nose down past the corners of a small full-lipped mouth and disappeared under the prominent jaw about an inch on either side of the deep cleft in the chin. A blue-black stubble so dense that it admitted no hint of skin seemed to grow before

Jack's eyes. Day's head was crowned by a wavy thatch of black hair that contained no gray. Jack wondered if he had ever seen such a sinister mug and decided that it was really no contest.

"I told Yeats that I only have a few minutes. Maybe you'd like to tell me what's on your mind."

"A friend of mine was murdered. I want to find out who's responsible. Quickly and quietly."

"That's usually a job for the police. And murder investigations are often neither quick nor quiet. The cops are not keen on private competition, Mr. Lee."

"I'm not particularly keen on the cops, Mr. Day. I need help and I'm willing to pay well for it. Shall I go on?"

"I'm listening."

"With off-the-record ears?"

"If that's the way you want it. I'll listen to what you have to say. If I can help you, fine. If I can't, I'll forget every word."

"Are you familiar with the Smiley murder?"

Day's eyes burned a bit brighter and he leaned forward across the booth.

"The guy they found hanging on the cross?"

Jack nodded.

"Hell yes, I'm familiar with it. So is half the world."

"Smiley was my friend. Whoever killed him took something very valuable. Something that I would like to recover for the sake of his wife and kids. I need to get to the murderer before the police do."

"You're out of your fucking mind."

"Have been for quite a while now. The fifty thousand dollar question is, are you? That's what I'm willing to pay if you can lead me to the asshole that did Smiley. You give it a serious shot and come up empty, I'll still spring for ten."

"What are you trying to recover?"

"Over a hundred pounds of top-shelf marijuana."

"And what happens if you get lucky and find this person?"

"That's none of your business. You're out of it at that point."

"You have any ideas where to start?"

"I'm doing a little bottom fishing with a pound of Smiley's herb for bait. Left it with a friend who knows about such things earlier this morning. That's it. I was hoping that you might have an ear in downtown. I know it's a long shot."

"I need to give this some thought. A lot of thought. How can I get in touch?"

Before Jack could answer, a waiter appeared and told Darrell Day that he had a phone call. From a lady.

When the detective returned, he did not sit down. Instead, he offered his hand and said, "I'm afraid we have a conflict of interests here. I'm not going to be able to help you. Sorry."

Jack shook the man's hand and watched him hurry out the back door. Then Jack walked out the front wondering what conflict of interest had appeared so suddenly in the course of Day's brief phone conversation.

A wave of fatigue washed over Jack as he stood in front of Manuel's and tried to decide what to do next. He felt aimless and lacking in resolution. Finally, he realized what he was avoiding.

He drove a few blocks over to Inman Park and

parked in front of a nicely restored two-storied house on Elizabeth Street. A white banner with a blue and red butterfly, symbol of the now-proud neighborhood whose residents had reclaimed it from the brink of neglectful ruin, fluttered from a metal pole attached to the front of the house. Jack walked around to the back and climbed the stairs that led to Deborah's apartment.

The small apartment was totally still, quiet in an almost absolute way. Jack walked through the spotless, tiny kitchen into a hallway that connected the living room, bath, and bedroom. He stopped in the hall and listened carefully. A sound so subtle as to be barely audible, a single, continuous hum that Jack thought of as the sound of time, filled his ears. After listening for a minute, he felt leaden of body and drowsy. Like a sleepwalker, he put one foot slowly in front of the other until he had reached the bedroom. He took off his shoes and stretched out, fully clothed, upon the bed. As soon as he closed his eyes, he began to drift. The feeling of falling slowly through space was his last awareness as he slipped gratefully into forgetful sleep.

Deborah O'Hara felt a relieved gladness in her heart when she saw Jack's truck parked in front of her house. She parked in her driveway and raced up the back steps. When she opened the door and felt the stillness, she took off her shoes and walked quietly through the apartment until she found Jack in the bedroom.

The peacefulness and serenity that had so attracted her to Jack were not evident on his sleeping face. Instead, she saw worry and trouble written there. She had felt him begin to pull away from her the moment that they had seen Smiley on television. As he pulled away, some frightening new quality that she couldn't define had begun to emerge in Jack. She felt that she was losing him so soon after having found him and was totally helpless to do anything about it.

Deborah walked around the bed and lay lightly beside Jack. When he opened his eyes, she gently closed them with the thumb and forefinger of her left hand and began to massage his temples.

"I was so happy to see your truck. When you left yesterday and said that you would call, I didn't think that I would be seeing you for a while."

Jack rolled over and took her in his arms. He breathed in the smell of her hair, felt the warmth of her willing body, and felt his resolve melting. With bitter regret, he pulled back until he could see her face.

"I have something to tell you. I didn't want to tell you on the telephone."

"I don't like the sound of this, Jack."

"We can't be together for a while. Until all of this business with Smiley is cleared up."

"I don't understand. All of what business?"

"Some things might happen that . . . well, there could be trouble. Trouble that you shouldn't be any part of. I can't explain. Trust me on this."

Deborah pulled away and sat up crosslegged on the bed. Hurt and anger played upon her face. Her hazel eyes filled with tears. A tremor passed over her lips as she began to speak.

"How can you say that to me? Two days ago we were planning a life. What are you doing, Jack? What are you planning to do that could possibly keep us apart? Is it more important than we are? Please don't do this. I'm scared for you and scared of losing you. Smiley's gone. Nothing that you can do is going to change that. We have a shot at something special. Let's take it, Jack. Please."

Jack was moved by both the words and the plea in her eyes. But the implacable thing that was growing in him remained untouched. He felt it, hard and unyielding, just behind his breastbone, and knew that he would be ruled by it until he had done what must be done.

"I can't explain. Anything that I said could implicate you in . . . I don't know what. I just know that this is something that I can't let go. I'm sorry."

"I'm sorry, too, Jack. I'm sorry and confused and hurt and I'm mad as hell at you and I think maybe you should leave now."

A cool breeze greeted Jack when he stepped out of the apartment. A feeling of relief grew with each step down the back stairs. He felt free to pursue the monster that waited out there for him. Driving back toward the ridge into the setting sun, he found himself wondering what manner of man he sought. I want you, he thought. God help me, I want you much more than I should.

At 11:45 Tuesday morning, Jack Lee stood beneath a shower head that rained forceful streams of near-scalding water down upon his shoulders and back. He had risen at dawn and taken a three-hour walk in the woods, then chopped firewood for forty-five minutes. He was lost in the hot water and the steam when a heavy knocking on the front door rudely snapped him out of his reverie.

Cursing, Jack stepped from the shower and wrapped a towel around his waist. On his way to the front door, he concocted some choice words for the lost hunter that he expected to find. He flung open the door and was amazed to find Darrell Day swaying unsteadily on the doorstep, a half-empty bottle of whiskey in one hand and a magazine in the other.

The man looked like he had slept in an industrial-sized clothes dryer set for maximum tumble. He wore the same clothes that Jack had seen him in the day before. His hair stood on end, as if he had recently been hooked up to Georgia Power. His bloodshot black eyes had gone from yesterday's sinister to full-on insane. The craggy face had grown a riot of new wrinkles, and the heavy beard had sprouted a black stubble capable of scraping raw bark from trees. He muttered under his breath as he glowered at Jack. When Jack opened the storm door, he reeled into the room, flung the magazine at Jack, and turned the bottle straight up. After three gurgling swallows he wiped his mouth with the back of his hand.

"It's a goddamn shitty world out there, bud. Full of stinking-ass murderous scum I'm here to tell you. You still looking for a murderer, Mr. Jack Lee?"

"I thought there was some kind of conflict of interest."

"There was. Not anymore. She got her goddamn ears chopped off last night."

"Who?"

"Courtney Fowler. That's who."

"The reporter?"

"Yeah. That was her on the phone yesterday at Manuel's. She hired me to check out a character named Reverend Clyde and somebody named Clint. She got an anonymous call. Caller told her these guys were in on the murders. Then hung up. I need to sit down."

Jack pointed him toward the sofa in front of the fireplace and excused himself to get dressed. He threw the magazine on the bed and looked over the cover while he buttoned his shirt. The magazine was MOUNTAIN LIFE. The cover contained a facial portrait of an elderly man with a shock of snow-white hair and a long, unkempt white beard that obscured the mouth. The feverish pale of his blue eyes was barely distinguishable from the whites. Spectacular white brows floated beneath a massive forehead that jutted out as far as the tip of his long, prominent nose. The face reminded Jack of an oil painting of *Zeus in Fury* that he had seen as a child.

"Hey, how did you find this place?" Jack called out into the living room.

When he got no answer, Jack returned to the living room and found Darrell Day passed out in a drunken sprawl. A pool of spittle had formed in the corner of his slack mouth. Deep, bubbling sounds accompanied each exhalation. Jack started to shake the man awake and then decided against it. Instead, he covered him with an old wool blanket and added a couple of sticks of wood to the fire. Then he took the magazine into the kitchen and turned to the story on Reverend Clyde Causey titled CONVERSATIONS WITH GOD.

When he put the magazine down thirty minutes later, Jack felt more impressed by what had been omitted from the article than by what had been contained therein. No mention had been made of Reverend Clyde Causey's past. The article began with a description of Reverend Clyde's arrival in Sugar Valley, Georgia, in

1986, his cash purchase of three hundred acres of land in the Snake Creek Gap area, and his founding of the Church of the Swift Sword from whose pulpit Reverend Clyde espoused a doctrine of white supremacy, self-reliance, and the purification of America, God's chosen nation. The massive, fortress-like field stone church had a seating capacity of seven hundred fifty people and had taken a year to build at a cost estimated to be over two and one-half million dollars. The article made no mention of the source of the funding for the purchase of the land or the building of the church. It was noted, however, that the church came well in advance of the congregation which, with the exception of a small nucleus of Reverend Clyde's followers, was nonexistent at the time of the completion of the church. At the time of the September 1990 article, the church had a membership of six hundred, two hundred of whom lived on church property.

The article quoted Reverend Clyde as saying that the source of his authority was none other than the Lord Jehovah, God of Moses and Father of Jesus Christ, who had spoken to him and commanded him to found a church and establish a community. According to Reverend Clyde, his every word and act was inspired by the direct word of God. In accordance with God's wishes, the Reverend brought one hundred acres of bottom land under intense cultivation and devoted one hundred acres to the keeping of livestock. These enterprises had made the community almost self-sufficient in terms of food. Solar technology and windmills had brought the community close to energy self-sufficiency. The stated goal of Reverend Clyde was total self-sufficiency in all areas of life by the year 1993. He predicted that from this seed enterprise would spring a network of church communities destined to become the dominant influence over every square inch of America. By the year 2000, he said, America would be a pure vessel filled with the faith of an all-white citizenry. He made no mention of the means for achieving this all-white America nor the fate of non-white Americans.

All male members of the community were required to participate in a program that taught community defense and survival tactics. A color photograph on the last page of the article showed a group of thirty men assembled in ranks of ten. All the men wore green camouflage clothing and held what appeared to be Colt AR-15's at port arms. In front of the group stood a tall, lean man in similar dress whose face was obscured by black and green camo paint. A caption below the photograph identified the man as Clint DuBois, Chief of Community Defense and Instructor of Survival Tactics. The only personal information given for DuBois indicated that he was a former Green Beret with combat experience in Vietnam.

Jack picked up the magazine and reread the paragraph at the end of the article. Two services weekly were open to the public. There was a prayer meeting each Wednesday evening at 7:00 and a Sunday morning service at 11:00. A potluck supper preceded the Wednesday prayer meeting at 6:00 P.M.

A loud, wheezing snore from the living room broke the silence. Jack went to check on Darrell Day and found him turned onto his right side, with his face mashed into the back of the couch in such a way that his nose was bent to the left, almost touching his cheek. Jack studied the man for a few moments and wondered why the death of Courtney Fowler had touched him so deeply. Best to let him sleep, he thought. We can talk when he's slept it off.

Jack warmed up some leftover black bean stew and cornbread and took a tray out to the deck. It was another superb fall day. The clear sky contained only a bright yellow sun which lit the carpet of autumn color covering the valley. Fifteen miles to the south the tricky light of the horizon gave a series of ridges the illusion of snowy caps. A flight of buzzards rode a thermal in languorous circles high above the center of the valley. Jack watched the buzzards and pondered the events that had overtaken him in the twenty-five days since he had broken his three-year retreat. The fandango of love and death that had followed his reemergence into the world seemed incredible, dreamlike. Was this crazy panorama unfolding before his eyes merely a grand illusion, the Maya of Hindu philosophy? If this is illusion, reality must be hell on wheels, he thought.

After he had finished his lunch, Jack returned to the kitchen and washed the dishes. Then he walked to the bedroom and stretched out on the bed. He lay still and watched his thoughts wander in the direction of Sugar Valley and Reverend Clyde and Clint DuBois. Just before he drifted into sleep, he heard the low hoot of an owl. Owls hooting at midday, he thought. The world has truly turned upside down.

* * *

Jack wakened slowly, rising to the waking surface through layer after layer of foggy sleep. He felt tired and unrefreshed, unwilling to face what lay ahead. He recognized the first signs of oncoming depression since the end of his trial. With effort, he forced himself to rise. The bright rays of the lowering sun shone through the west window of the bedroom, illuminating dancing motes of dust. The dead quiet in the cabin told Jack that Darrell Day was still asleep.

Jack walked to the bathroom and splashed cold water on his face. When he lowered the towel from his face and saw his reflection in the mirror, he detected not a trace of happiness.

He found Day asleep on his stomach when he walked through the living room toward the kitchen. He deliberated whether to grind fresh coffee beans in the noisy machine and decided in favor of the idea. When the noise from the machine abated, a low moan arose from the living room.

Jack walked into the living room and found Darrell Day sitting up with his hands covering his face.

"Coffee?"

Day removed his hands from his face, exposing the visage of a gargoyle.

"Yeah, thanks. What time is it?"

"A little after 4:00."

"Jesus."

Jack poured coffee into two tall ceramic mugs, doctored his own with half and half and honey, and walked back to the fireplace. He placed Day's mug on the table in front of the sofa and watched as Day poured a healthy slug of bourbon into his cup from the half-empty bottle of Maker's Mark.

"Hair of the dog," Day said, offering Jack the bottle.

Jack shook his head in refusal and waited.

"Sorry to show up on your doorstep in this condition. Guess I went a little loco when I heard about Courtney."

"No problem. How did you find me?"

"I talked to Yeats Murphy. He gave decent directions and I still got lost. Ended up way the hell back in the woods."

"Feel up to a little fresh air?"

"Sure, might do some good."

They stood quietly for a while on the deck, drinking coffee and taking in the view. A light wind blew in from the west, rattling the colorful leaves that would soon fall from the trees.

"This is a beautiful spot. Peaceful. Somehow not what I expected from the reincarnation of Rhett Butler."

"Give me a break, Mr. Day."

"Darrell. And I'm gonna call you Jack if you don't mind."

"Fine. I'd like to hear what you drove all the way out here to say."

"I got a call from my secretary at 6:00 this morning about Courtney. She told me to turn on the TV. Apparently, Courtney was found by Tom Doyle about midnight last night in the bedroom of his apartment. She was tied to a chair, dead. No ears. A lot of burns from neck to waist on the front of her body. A single gunshot wound between the eyes from a small caliber weapon. Extremely close range. Same M.O., same signature as the O'Dell and Cole killings. According to Doyle, she had moved into his place as a safety precaution."

"I'm sorry to hear about Miss Fowler. You were close?"

"We had worked together. She used me on an investigation of the state legislature and we hit it off. She was about my daughter's age. Very bright. Beautiful. Ambitious as hell. She had lost her dad about the time we met. We kind of fell into one of those surrogate relationships. Maybe something like you and Yeats, huh?"

"Maybe. Just how much did Yeats tell you about me?"

"Enough for me to consider trusting you. I've known Yeats for quite a while now and I've never known him to be wrong about anyone yet."

"He spoke highly of you, too. That's good enough for me. Yesterday's offer still stands."

Darrell turned on Jack and gave him a withering look.

"Yesterday's history. This is personal now. I want to see whoever is responsible for this brought down. All the way down."

"You think this call that Courtney got is for real?"

"I don't know, but it's the only place I know to start. She had a feeling about it and her instincts were damn good."

"Why don't you take it to the cops?"

"Like I said, I want whoever did this burned down. I've seen a lot of investigations go nowhere or, even worse, lead to half-hearted prosecutions, plea bargained prison terms, even acquittal. You don't mind me saying so, I saw something in you yesterday that tells me you have something more basic in mind. That and the fact that Yeats is worried as hell about you. He says that you're capable of anything. Wants me to keep an eye on you. Well, I have no intention of trying to dissuade you from your revenge or whatever the hell it is that you want. Am I reaching you here?"

"Loud and clear. Since you seem to know more about my plans than I do, maybe you'd like to tell me what YOU have in mind."

"OK, I'll start at the top. When I met Courtney yesterday afternoon at 2:30, she had just finished lunch with special agent Tommy Dalton of the GBI. The guy was pressing her hard, thought that she might be on to something and holding out on him. She wasn't having any, told him nicely that she was just as much in the dark as he was and to back off. I'm pretty sure that the law is sucking wind on this, too. Whoever is doing this is clever, leaves nothing behind to go on."

"Why was Courtney holding out on the boys?"

"I told you this is a very ambitious lady. She doesn't like Dalton's hard sell and she's got Pulitzer in her eyes. So we meet and she fills me in on this call she got. I check around with a couple of friends in the religion business and ask about a character called Reverend Clyde. One guy says 'Yeah, there's this weird old guy up in the mountains and wait a minute, I think I've got a magazine laying around here,' and he gives me the name of the magazine. I spend a little time in the library; read the article; see Clint DuBois's name and picture. So, we got Reverend Clyde and Clint, just like the caller mentioned.

"Then I call an old buddy in the Bureau who's on the task force for hate groups, cults, and the like. Ask him about this Church of the Swift Sword. He tells me that they are on the list but kind of an unknown quantity. Hard to penetrate. They've got guys on the edge, but nobody on the inside. So I make some more calls, start doing backgrounds on these two guys. I'll probably have something by Thursday.

"Meanwhile, the question is—was that call to Courtney for real or some crank? My gut says it was for real. My gut also tells me that Doc Cole made that call after his patient O'Dell spilled his guts to him. I mean, all these people were tortured. For what?"

"To find out if each person told anyone else after finding out about the murders."

"Yeats said you have a head on your shoulders. So, you've got O'Dell linked to Smiley. O'Dell linked to Doc Cole. A maybe on Doc Cole to Courtney."

"And Courtney to you."

"There is that."

"So, if Courtney mentioned telling you, you're next."

"Seems logical."

"All of it makes sense except Smiley. Why Smiley?"

"The only obvious thing is the pot. If it was just for the money, why not take it all? If we can figure out who, we'll find out why. Right now, we need one of us to make a visit to Sugar Valley and check out Reverend Clyde. My face is pretty well known in law enforcement circles and there's a good chance of agents in place up there. That leaves you, partner."

"I was thinking about making prayer meeting tomorrow night."

"You believe in God?"

"I don't know. Right now I'd say if there's a God, He's a knuckle ball pitcher and Phil Niekro is his only begotten Son."

For the first time since Jack had met him, Darrell

Day smiled. It was not a pretty sight.

"I think we're gonna get along, Jack. What time are you planning to head up?

"There's a potluck supper before the service. Thought I might break bread with the brethren and digest it with fire and brimstone. I'd like to get up there by 4:00 and take a look around."

"Look, I'm gonna hang around my house and play with my computer, wait for some calls. If the ear surgeon comes calling, I want to be there for him. Give me a call around noon just in case something breaks by then."

Day wrote something on a notepad, tore out a sheet, handed it to Jack. It contained a phone number and an address on Northside Drive.

"I'll call between 12:00 and 12:30. Your car down at the gate?"

"Yeah. I about ruptured myself climbing over that fucker."

"Come on, I'll walk down with you and unlock it."

They walked the six hundred feet to the gate in silence. Jack's mind tried to wrap itself around the fact that he was teaming up with the FBI. A fucking career G-Man. When they reached the gate, Day chuckled softly.

"A knuckle ball pitcher, huh?"

Jack unlocked the gate and held his hand out to Darrell.

"I never thought the sun would shine on this day, G-Man. Partner."

Amusement fought bitterness for equal time in Darrell's eyes as he shook Jack's hand firmly.

"Keep your head down and your powder dry, Rhett."

"Get outa here."

Back at the cabin, Jack sat for meditation. His mind emptied easily and he soon glided to the heart of silence, between the breaths where everything stops. Just before the timer signaled the end of the hour, a vision arose in his mind so terrible that he was wrenched from meditation, gasping as if awakened from a nightmare.

Shaken by what he had seen, Jack took the bottle of bourbon that Darrell had left and sat down on a lounge chair on the deck. He hooked a shot from the neck and wondered how much whiskey would be needed to get through what lay ahead.

A three-quarter moon, stark and silver, rose in the eastern sky. Jack sat bathed in the hard light for a long while sipping the whiskey. As he moved to rise for bed, a star fell from the heavens with a glorious tri-colored streak of green, yellow, and blue. Jack refrained from making a wish for fear that it might come true.

CHAPTER 13

At 3:42 Wednesday morning, Darrell Day was awakened by the clicking toenails of Rommell, his German Shepherd, on the hardwood floor of his bedroom. The dog was pacing in front of the sliding glass doors that led to the patio in the back yard. Rommell's high whine was different from the usual sound that indicated his desire to go out for toilet patrol. The sense of urgency in the dog's voice brought Darrell quickly to full consciousness. He quietly swung his legs over the side of the bed and felt about the floor until he located his bedroom slippers. He found his .45 Colt automatic with his right hand and a nine cell magnesium flashlight with his left. Slowly he stood and listened. A faint rasping sound emanated from the garage area at the other end of the house.

When Darrell reached the glass doors, he felt the rhythmic, metronomic swish of Rommell's tail against his leg. He quietly commanded the dog to heel and carefully unlocked the door. He slid the door open six inches and felt a blast of cold air hit his face. Rommell tensed against his left leg. When he heard the garage door begin to slide on its tracks, he opened the door and released Rommell. A low rumble came from Rommell's throat as he raced for the far end of the house. The waxing moon afforded just enough light for Darrell to see the dog turn the corner of the house. He followed the dog in a walking crouch with the .45 extended and the flashlight held by the bulb end next to his left ear, with his finger on the button switch. He had taken less than half a dozen steps when a howl of pain pierced the night for several seconds.

Darrell raced toward the end of the house and stopped when he reached the corner of the garage. He put his cheek against the cold brick wall, leaned forward until he reached the corner, and peered cautiously around it. A black-clad figure slipped out of the garage and around the opposite corner. Darrell had taken two steps in pursuit when the moonlight flashed on metal from the corner where the black figure had just disappeared. Darrell hit the deck on his belly. A silenced weapon uttered three fart-sighs. Darrell heard two bullets thud into the wood of the garage door frame just behind him. The last one ricocheted off the inner brick wall of the garage and hit a window on the car.

The sound of running feet brought Darrell to his own. He turned the corner from which the shots had come and heard a rattle from the chain-link fence at the far end of the house. He moved with quick, quiet strides toward the sound, stopping halfway to the fence to listen. Hearing nothing, he shined the light along the fence line. Nothing. He looked about him at the neighboring houses and saw that no lights had come on. All was quiet. The ear surgeon moves well, he thought.

When he turned on the garage light, Darrell found Rommell in a pool of blood. The dog's throat was laid open by a deep gash. Darrell studied the wound. The weapon had to be extremely sharp to penetrate Rommell's deep fur. Something like a straight razor.

Darrell went into the house and found an old

blanket. He slid the dog onto the blanket, dragging him by his back paws. Then he carried the animal that had been his best friend for five years to a secluded, tree-shrouded corner of the back yard. As he walked, he felt his own blood getting up to the danger point. He laid the dog gently on the ground and stood over him for several minutes, taking deep breaths and trying to control the anger that had his heart thudding.

After mopping the garage floor, Darrell went into the kitchen and put on a pot of coffee. While the coffee was brewing, he went out to his tool shed and removed a mattock and shovel, which he set down beside the patio. Then he placed the coffeepot, a cup, a bottle of Maker's Mark, and his .45 on a tray. He took the tray to the patio, placed it on a round cast-iron table, and sat down. After pouring equal measures of coffee and bourbon into his cup, Darrell Day sat back and waited for the first light, when he would bury his dog.

CHAPTER 14

Jack Lee awoke from an erotic dream early Wednesday morning. He had a huge erection and a dull pain in his testicles. He touched his throbbing member and considered giving himself relief. Instead, he rose and went to the bathroom to urinate. As his water met the water in the bowl, he closed his eyes and recaptured the image of Deborah's face beneath him in the dream. His desire for her had begun to take the form of a non-specific physical ailment. He had a case of what his grandmother used to call THE ALL OVERS.

After brewing a pot of Earl Grey tea, he sat at the kitchen table with a map of Georgia and located Sugar Valley. It lay about eighty miles northwest of Atlanta, just off I-75 on the eastern edge of a large section of the Chattahoochee National Forest. Jack noted with interest a recreation area with campsites less than ten miles from Sugar Valley in a place designated The Pocket. The name called out to him and he decided to take his camping gear with him and spend the night if there was no reason not to.

When he had finished his tea, Jack slipped on some jeans and a flannel shirt and drove the five miles to the nearest pay phone. The Thin Man answered on the second ring and told him there was nothing to report. He told Jack that he had some late business that evening and asked Jack to wait until noon the next day to call.

On his way home, Jack passed a large field of kudzu gleaming with sunlit dew. A black billy goat stood by the roadside grazing on the wet leaves hanging like green diamonds from the vines. When Jack drove past, the goat raised his horned head and contemplated him with calm yellow eyes. Then it shook its head in a way that seemed to Jack a sage warning. He felt a vague disquiet move through him and pass.

After a large breakfast of home-fried potatoes with onions and garlic, toasted whole wheat bread with melted Jack cheese, and two glasses of milk, Jack loaded up his camping gear, some extra clothes, and his Dop kit and headed for Atlanta. The high pressure that had dominated for the past several days was holding strong with a cloudless blue sky and high visibility. As he drove north on Highway 100 over the western shoulder of Blackjack Mountain, Mt. Cheaha, the highest peak in Alabama, stood in sharp relief, sixty miles away, against the western horizon. At I-20, he headed east and joined the thin trickle of traffic that breezed along at 70 miles per hour. Jack drove the sixty miles to Moreland Avenue on automatic pilot. He realized as he exited on North Moreland that he was unable to recollect a single thought from the past hour. Better wake up, boy, he thought.

At Little Five Points, Jack turned left onto Euclid and parked in the parking lot of Sevananda Natural Foods Co-op. A black dude with extravagant dreadlocks was playing a bamboo flute in front of the store. On the sidewalk at his feet, a collection of flutes for sale lay on a brightly colored cloth. When Jack walked by he said, "Hey brutha, deese flutes some kinda fine?"

"Jamaican?" Jack asked.

"No, brutha. Trinidad," the man said with a look of mock pain.

Inside, Jack bought loaves of whole wheat and black bread, goat cheese, black and green olives, two cans of vegetarian chili, two gallons of spring water, a selection of fruit, and several huge Tree of Life peanut butter cookies. After storing the supplies in the truck, he walked over to Calcutta restaurant.

Marveling at his own appetite, Jack ordered a vegetarian dinner from the evening menu for himself and a chicken birianie to go. When he stepped onto the street forty-five minutes later, he felt fortified for whatever might come against him.

When he handed the to-go containers to the flute player, the man sniffed them and made a face of approval.

"What's Dis, mon?"

"Fuel for the flute."

The man reached down and set the food on the cloth. When he straightened up, he held a small flute out to Jack. Jack tried to refuse. He knew that the man was not in the position to give anything away.

"Yes, mon. One good ting deserve another."

Jack smiled at the man and took the flute. The man from Trinidad gave him a pearl-white smile that spoke of a personal pride and dignity that the mean streets of America had not been able to rob. Jack nodded and knew that he had come away the richer in the exchange.

Strange morning, he thought as he walked toward the pay phone outside the Euclid Yacht Club. Black goats and dreadlocks and X-rated dreams.

Darrell Day answered before the end of the first ring. The hello that he uttered sounded more like a challenge than a greeting.

"Sounds like both sides of the bed were wrong this morning," Jack said.

"Are you in town?"

"Yeah. I'm in Little Five Points."

"You have my address with you?"

"Yes."

"May be a good idea for you to drop by before you head north. Come up on I-75 to Mt. Paran—take that to Northside and hang a left—it's a couple of blocks—number's on the mailbox. How soon can you get here?"

"I'm on the way. See you in twenty minutes."

* * *

Jack turned into the driveway and stopped for a moment to admire the two large magnolias that dominated the front yard that ran from the curb to the split-level brick house situated on the top and south slope of a small knoll. He parked just outside the open garage door, behind a black Chrysler LeBaron. As he stepped from the truck, the door connecting the garage with the house opened and Darrell Day motioned him in. A small hole surrounded by sunburst fractures in the right rear window of the Chrysler caught his attention when he walked through the garage. He looked up at Darrell Day with questioning eyes and received a curt nod in return.

Jack stepped into the kitchen and studied Darrel Day's haggard face in the full light of the fluorescent fixture. He looked worse than he had the day before. Black smudges hung like decayed half-moons under his tired, bloodshot eyes. The grim set of his jaw was the only firm feature on a face that had collapsed upon itself in a cascade of wrinkles. When he spoke, weariness weighted his words.

"He was here."

"Last night?" Jack asked.

"About 3:45 this morning. Come on, we'll sit outside."

Jack followed Darrell through the kitchen and out onto a fieldstone patio that ran the length of the house and extended twenty feet into the large backyard. In the left corner of the yard was a mound of fresh earth. Darrell looked from Jack to the grave.

"The son of a bitch killed my dog, Rhett. I'm going to miss that dog more than I did my wife when she left me."

"Did you get a look at him?"

"Too dark. And I was too busy dodging bullets."

They sat down at the cast-iron table. Jack noticed an ashtray in which two flattened pieces of metal gleamed like a pair of dead eyes.

"I dug these out of the garage door frame this morning, .22 caliber. I'm lucky they weren't dug out of me."

"You call the cops?"

"No. And neither did the neighbors 'cause they didn't hear a thing. Our boy carried a silenced .22, the assassin's choice. Whoever this guy is, he's pretty good."

Jack listened quietly while Darrell recounted the entire episode. When he had finished, Darrell rose from his chair and motioned for Jack to follow him. They entered Darrell's bedroom through the sliding glass doors and proceeded to a hallway that ended at a door at the other end of the house. Darrell opened the door and led Jack into a small room crammed full of computer equipment and filing cabinets. On a large desk in front of a picture window overlooking the front yard sat a modem, a fax machine, and two manila folders. On the top folder, the name of Reverend Clyde Causey was printed in red ink on a strip of contact tape. Darrell picked up the folders and handed them to Jack.

The folder on Reverend Clyde contained sixty-seven pages and Clint DuBois's had twenty-three. Jack was surprised and impressed.

"Damn, you work pretty quick," Jack said.

"Tools of the trade and the right connections," Darrell said with a tired wave of his right hand toward the equipment behind him.

"Plus motivation. Killing a man's dog is enough to piss a body off."

"Look, I need to get on the road fairly soon. Think you could distill this into a couple of thousand words or less?"

"I don't know if I can do these two wackos justice with that few words but I'll give it a go. Let's do it over coffee."

Jack sat at the kitchen counter and accepted a large mug of coffee. Darrell began to pace the kitchen floor.

"Well, let's see, I guess I'll start with age before beauty. Although, make no mistake, both of these dudes are beauts, for a fact.

"Clyde Augustus Causey was born in 1922 to Noble and Emma Causey in Macon, Georgia. Noble made a fortune in the cotton business, amassing huge land holdings and gin facilities throughout the state in the process.

When young Clyde was ten, Emma Causey went insane and was institutionalized, following in the footsteps of her mother and older sister. She died in the institution in 1972.

"Noble Causey reared his son with the help of his younger sister Maude, a deeply religious spinster who moved into the family home after Emma's incarceration. She apparently had a deep influence on Clyde, who became something of a phenomenon as a child preacher under her tutelage. Clyde's psychiatric records indicate that he was emotionally distanced from his father from the time of Emma's death.

"In 1940, at the age of eighteen, Clyde went directly from high school to The Baptist Seminary in Knoxville, Tennessee. This is where it gets good.

"In his second year at the seminary, Clyde began to preach impromptu sermons in which he characterized the members of the seminary faculty as Scribes and Pharisees, blasphemers, and general perverters of the true message of Christ. He was suspended for a period of three months, at the end of which he was reinstated. His reinstatement coincided with a large donation to the seminary from his father.

"Shortly after his reinstatement, Clyde resumed his abusive sermonizing and was permanently expelled. On the Sunday following his expulsion, Clyde appeared on the steps of the seminary chapel during services. Upon having their service disrupted by his loud ranting, the congregation opened the doors to find Clyde Causey naked, bleeding from the side, and bearing a large wooden cross. In a severe snowstorm, no less.

"After several minutes of verbal abuse characterized

by witnesses as 'depraved profanity,' Clyde was physically restrained and delivered to a local hospital. Subsequently, he was installed by his father in a private sanitarium outside Macon. Shortly after his arrival there, he mauled an attendant, inflicting numerous severe bite wounds which later became infected and nearly caused the death of the man he had attacked. He was kept in restraint for two years and then released to close confinement in his room. He remained in close confinement until one year prior to his release in 1983."

"He was locked up for forty years?" Jack asked.

"Without visitors. Clyde consistently refused the visits of his father who in turn forbade the aunt, Maude, to visit him. Noble came to blame the boy's condition on the overzealous religious training of Maude.

"What was his condition? The diagnosis?" Jack asked.

"You name it. During the course of his stay, Clyde was variously diagnosed as paranoid-schizophrenic, cyclical manic-depressive, and every other label that came into vogue during those forty years. His symptoms ran the gamut: voices, delusions, intense paranoia, Christ identification, self-destructive acts. Finally, he lapsed into an autistic state. For ten of the eleven years prior to his release, he did not utter a word or acknowledge the world around him. When his father died in 1982, conservatorship passed to his Aunt Maude, his last remaining relative. His autism ended at the time of her first visit. From that moment, he began what seemed to be a miraculous recovery. A year later he was released into her custody and moved back to his ancestral home. When Aunt Maude passed in 1985, Clyde inherited an estate worth seventeen million dollars. One year later he shows up in Sugar Valley."

"You feel reasonably confident of the accuracy of all of this?"

"If you remember, I told you yesterday that I have an old friend with the Bureau who is part of the task force on hate groups, cults, etc. These guys do extensive background workups on the leaders of these groups. So, yeah, I think that this is fairly high quality intelligence. There's a lot here that I skipped over, but you got the high points."

"Sounds like a case of bad seed. A strain of madness on the mother's side."

"Well, my psychiatric qualifications are slight, but it does seem that there's a genetic component working here. You can read the whole report when you return from visiting the good reverend."

"OK. What's the skinny on Clint DuBois?"

"We can title this one ENTER THE PSYCOPATH. Clinton William DuBois was born to Amanda and Robert DuBois in Gainesville, Georgia. Robert abandoned mother and child shortly after Clint's birth. Miss Amanda never remarried and went on to enjoy a career as something of a loose woman.

"Young Clint began to amass a long list of disciplinary problems from the time he entered school. Although his IQ was measured at 145, he performed poorly in school and demonstrated strong antisocial tendencies. He was expelled from school several times for fighting, particularly in junior high. He quit school on the first day he could legally do so. Within a month, he had his first arrest for theft. This was followed by a string of petty offenses, juvenile courts, and probated sentences. He was brought up on charges of poisoning several of his neighbors' dogs and found innocent.

"At the age of fifteen, Clint went after his mother and one of her johns with a butcher knife. They were both carved up pretty well, although both subsequently recovered. For this, Clint was sentenced to three years in Alto, the maximum security boy's reformatory. This place is straight out of Dickens. Clint became a model inmate, received his high school equivalency diploma, and was released in 1966 at the age of eighteen. A month later, Clint was in the army.

"After basic and AIT, Clint was shipped out to Vietnam. After a combat tour on the ground, he re-upped for a second tour, this time as a door gunner on a chopper. Toward the end of the second tour, he was wounded in the leg and shipped stateside for recovery. Six months later he was accepted for Special Forces training and was soon back in Nam for his third tour.

"Things get a little fuzzy here. Midway through his third tour, Clint disappeared into the bush and didn't show up again for three months, at which time he was immediately shipped back to the states and detained for eighteen months, ostensibly for combat fatigue. I say ostensibly because *combat fatigue* is a term used to cover a wide range of irregularities that don't show up on official records. There is no mention of the facility where he was detained nor of any specific treatment program. He received an honorable discharge after his release in 1971.

"From 1971 until 1986, when he shows up with Reverend Clyde in Sugar Valley, there is a total blank.

No tax records, no W2's, voting records, insurance data, nada."

"What do you make of this disappearance in Nam and the eighteen month detention? Was that kind of thing normal?"

"Normal? No. I don't know what to think of it. I've got an old friend with army intelligence digging deeper on that for me. Old Clint's a regular mystery man."

"Maybe I can get a look at him tonight."

"Speaking of tonight, take it real easy. No questions, no digging around. Don't volunteer any information about yourself to anyone. Just observe and get back to me tomorrow. Say noon?"

"Perfect. I've got to check back with my friend who's watching the street for Smiley's herb about then. I'll call you right after that."

"Nothing yet on that, huh?"

"Zip, but it's a little early yet. How about you? You look rough, man. I was planning to camp in the mountains tonight but I could come back down and sit up while you get some sleep. You might get another visit."

"Thanks, but you go ahead. I've got a friend coming over this afternoon and I'll get some shut-eye then. I have a feeling the ear surgeon won't make his next move here."

Darrell walked Jack out to his truck and stood at the top of the driveway. His arms hung limply at his sides and his head was partially bowed. As Jack was backing down the driveway, he looked up and saw Darrell's right arm rise slowly in a half-hearted goodbye, a gesture which brought Jack his first feeling of warmth for Darrell Day.

Chapter 15

At 3:25 P.M., Jack crossed the murky red Oostanaula River, which separates the small mountain town of Calhoun from the community of Sugar Valley. As he descended into the valley, Jack saw that a tall continuous mountain ridge formed the western boundary. At the north end of the valley, another long ridge ran back to the southeast. The southern ridge from which Jack descended formed the third wall of the three-sided valley, the flat bottom of which spread for several miles in all directions. A sprinkling of small farms and homes gave the valley an underpopulated look. The freshly turned fields of some of the farms exposed deep-red fertile soil

Jack found that Sugar Valley proper was less than a town and more than a crossroad. Close by the tracks of a railroad crossing, a small textile mill, two country stores, and several short streets lined with wood frame houses formed the nucleus of the community. Traveling north, Jack passed an old country school built of field stone that, from its look of disuse, had long since seen its last student. Farther along, a surprisingly large Baptist church in immaculate repair testified that the community took its religion seriously. Jack found it difficult to reconcile this pastoral setting with the presence of a hate-mongering outfit like Reverend Clyde's.

Just past the church, Jack came to a well-tended cemetery that had the appearance of considerable age about it. He pulled over to the side of the road and got out to stretch his legs. The cemetery was situated on a small hill with the names Watkins, Walraven, DeFoor, Holsumback, and Brown on large marble markers. Fresh flowers decorated several of the graves. The obvious love and respect shown to the dead again gave Jack pause to wonder about the presence of The Church of the Swift Sword in this beautiful little valley.

Jack traveled north for ten miles and decided when he hit the far side of Snake Creek Gap that he must have missed the sign for the turn-off to Reverend Clyde's property. He backtracked and again missed the sign mentioned in the MOUNTAIN LIFE article. Confused, Jack pulled into the parking lot of an ancient country store at the south end of Snake Creek Gap. The old building was made of weathered heart pine and covered with a roof of rusted tin. Looking at the store, Jack experienced a mild feeling of vertigo. Each wall of the building leaned in a different direction in defiance of gravity. The tin roof seemed ready to fall through the middle of the store at the touch of the next brisk wind. The boards of the porch sagged toward the middle, forming a one-foot depression just below the front door. The skewed confluence of angles gave the appearance that the building was moving before Jack's eyes. An old white sign with Coca-Cola logos on either end stood over the doorway and informed the world that this was DeFoor's General Store.

When Jack climbed the steps and reached the front door, the boards sagged dangerously another few inches under his weight. As he stepped cautiously into the store, he looked back at the porch to see if it had given way. From behind him a merry, lilting laughter arose.

"Don't worry your head, boy. Ole Mrs. Brown weighs three hundred pounds and hadn't fallen through yet."

Jack turned and saw an old man sitting in a rocker beside a potbelly stove. The man's bald head bobbed up and down and his wizened face held a devilish look of mirth. His startling green eyes shone with an innocent, childlike intensity, as if lit by a pure inner light. He wore an old black and green wool shirt with rolled-up sleeves exposing a thermal undershirt. His bib overalls were patched and shiny. His brogans had made a long career of avoiding polish. He looked more comfortable and at peace with himself than any human being Jack had ever encountered.

"Afternoon. I was hoping you could give me some directions."

"What exactly is it you're lookin' for?"

"Well, according to the directions I have, there's supposed to be a sign for the Church of the Swift Sword just north of here on the left."

"Yep," said the old man. The humor had left his face and his narrowed eyes had a look of wary appraisal.

"Unless I'm going blind, there's no sign."

"Nope."

"I'd appreciate it if you could help me out with some directions."

The old man rose gracefully from his rocker and walked to within six inches of Jack. His bright green eyes sought and held Jack's for a long moment.

"You don't look like one of them, boy. But if you

are, you'd best be leavin' 'cause them people ain't welcome here."

Jack noticed that the man's hands had slipped into his pockets as he spoke. He felt sure that there was a pistol in one of those deep pockets, and the look on the old man's face told him that it could be brought into play without a second thought.

"I'm not one of them, sir. I'm just up here on some private business."

"You'll have to forgive me, son," the old man said shaking his head.

"That place up there is a cancer on this valley and those folks have got me 'bout fit to be tied. I've lived here all my born days and that bunch up there is the worst thing I've yet to see."

"It sounds like a rough outfit," Jack said sympathetically.

"You don't even know the half of it. Look, I've done gone and forgot my manners. I'm LaFayette DeFoor. Friends call me Fate."

Jack shook the offered hand and found surprising strength in it. He wondered whether to give the old man his real name and decided that it would be unwise to be anything less than truthful. He felt an instant trust for Fate DeFoor and had a feeling that this old fellow had turned the tables on more than a few slickers in his day.

"I'm Jack Lee, Fate. Pleased to meet you."

"You got time to drink a Co-Cola?"

"Thank you. I do have a thirst."

"Have a seat," Fate said, motioning to the rocker beside his own.

Fate returned from the vintage Coca-Cola cooler

with two short bottles of Coke and sat down. He handed one bottle to Jack and smiled.

"Now you was wantin' some directions to the Devil's roost. Funny thing about that sign. Seems to disappear 'bout as fast as they can replace it."

"Do the other people in the valley feel the way you do about them?"

"Seems to be a matter of how close folks live to 'em, not that anybody cares much for the whole lot. Now me, for instance, I live right next door to 'em. So, I guess you could say I've got the most call for hard feelin's. How 'bout you. What brings you up our way?"

"Well, let's just say I heard a little about Reverend Clyde's conversations with God and wanted to check him out for myself."

Fate DeFoor rose and walked to the door.

"That's a fine old truck you've got there. Apache, ain't it?"

"Yes, sir."

"Used to have one just like it when I was a younger man. Bought it brand new in '56. Mind if I take a look at it?"

"Not at all."

They walked out to the old truck and saw three beat-up looking cars traveling close together in the north-bound lane. Each car was jam-packed with men, women, and children.

"There goes some of 'em now. Reverend Clyde brings in half the white trash around here to these damn meetin's of his. You headin' up to that prayer meetin' tonight?"

"Thought I might take a look around."

"You know, Jack Lee, something tells me you're not up here to aid the reverend's cause. You got time to take a spin? I'd sure fancy a ride in this old girl."

Jack reached into his pocket and pulled out his keys. He threw them into the air a foot, caught them with his right hand, then threw them across the hood to Fate.

"Just give me a minute to hang a sign on the door."

Fate reached inside the door and withdrew a cardboard sign. He closed the door, impaled the sign on a nail, and straightened it to his liking. BE BACK SOON was printed in an uneven, childlike fashion. The best Jack could tell, Fate had not locked the door.

When Fate climbed behind the wheel, he puzzled over the gear selector mounted on the steering column.

"Automatic?"

"Yeah, I had a friend put it in when he dropped in the new engine."

Fate turned the ignition key and sat back and looked at Jack when the engine rumbled to life, sending a tremor through the truck.

"Whoa! What in the blue blazes you got under that dang hood, boy?"

"A 350 V-8. Think you can handle it?"

"Hah! You just hang on."

Fate made a U-turn in the parking lot and barreled north into Snake Creek Gap. After a half mile, he slowed and pointed to a mailbox on the left. A two-rut road met the highway a few feet from the box.

"My place is a little ways back in there."

Jack saw nothing but woods.

"Cain't see the house from the road. Now right

there is where that sign you was lookin' for used to be."

At the end of a long gravel driveway, the stumps of two treated poles had been sawed off near ground level, apparently recently cut.

"The church is back in there?"

"Yep. They gottum a little guard house set up just inside that tree line just so's you cain't see it from the road. You'll pass inspection before you get in there."

"So they have pretty tight security?"

"Security's what they call it. I call it something else. Look, it's too purdy a day to spend talkin' 'bout them varmits. You'll get an earful of that tonight. I was thinkin' to make a quick loop up through The Pocket—show you a nice piece of country. Just take thirty minutes."

"I've got time. As a matter of fact, I was thinking about camping at that campground in The Pocket."

"I saw your gear in the back of the truck. Fact is, the campground's closed for the season. I got a little side pasture you might find to your likin'. Show it to you later."

Since passing a boundary sign for the Chattahoochee National Forest, they had been climbing steadily. Fate settled into a nice fifty-mile-an-hour pace and hummed softly to himself. The crisp autumn air took on a bracing chill as they gained altitude. The foliage had reached absolute peak, painting the mountains in living color beyond capture by any master's palette.

Shortly after the road began to wind to the west, Fate turned left on The Pocket Road. They headed south, paralleling the Sugar Valley Road, which lay unseen on their left, hundreds of feet below. On their right, a fiery sun had begun its descent in the western sky, dropping toward the peak of another long mountain ridge.

"On the right, there, that's John's Mountain. Horn Mountain on our left. The Pocket here is smack in between. Runs for miles and miles. It's plumb wild up here, like the good Lord intended."

Jack nodded. Except for a few old houses here and there, there was little sign of human life. They had not passed another car for miles.

Fate pulled into a small clearing on the left.

"Over there," he said, pointing toward the edge of the clearing. "There's an old trail that runs clean down to my place. Down to Thigh Bone Cave on Reverend Clyde's place, too."

"Thigh Bone Cave?"

"Yeah, that's where the Reverend does his talkin' to God. So he says. The old coot spends days at a time prayin' an fastin' up there. Place got its name when one of them arkyolygists found a human thigh bone in it a few years back. Run some kinda tests on it. Said it was four or five hunnert years old or some such."

As they negotiated a long curve, a vista opened, exposing the crooked peak of a tall mountain.

"What's that tall mountain over there?"

"That there is Horn Mountain, where we're aheadin'. In the war between the states, one of my mother's people, a Watkins woman, walked over that mountain and clear over to Resaca for salt. These people here was desperate for salt. Even boiled the dirt from the smokehouses to git it."

When they reached the top of the mountain, Fate parked the truck in a turn-around and made a sweeping gesture with his right hand.

"Now that's some view, ain't it?"

They got out of the truck and stood on the edge of the peak in the whipping wind. To the west, Jack could see clearly The Pocket running between the mountains for many miles. To the east, Sugar Valley lay far below them like some hidden, mythical Shangri-La. Jack was a little stunned by the grandeur of the view and puzzled that he had never before heard of this place.

"I been seein' this all my life and it still gets to me. Whaddya think, Jack Lee?"

"It's really beautiful, Fate. I think that I owe you thanks for showing it to me."

"Think nothin' of it. 'Preciate you lettin' me drive that truck. Guess we'd best be moseyin' on back now."

They drove down the steep east side of Horn Mountain and arrived at the Sugar Valley Road where it crossed the railroad tracks in the heart of the little community. Fate turned left and retraced Jack's original route into the valley. When they reached the store, Fate turned off the ignition and sat back in the seat.

"Well sir, I enjoyed that a right smart. Tell you what, when you get shut of them people up there, drop by my place. I'd be proud to put you up for the night. Nobody there but me, and to tell the truth, I'd enjoy the company. Lessin' of course you got other plans."

There was not a disingenuous bone in the old man's body. Jack liked Fate's company and the offer was a welcomed respite.

"If you're sure it wouldn't be an inconvenience, I'll take you up on that, Fate."

"No trouble a'tall. We might even crack a jug and

swap a few yarns."

"Do you have a room in the store that I might use to change clothes?"

"Sure 'nough. Come on in."

Fifteen minutes later, Jack walked out of the store wearing a slightly frayed white shirt open at the collar, an old tweed sport coat with almost worn-through elbows, jeans, and a scruffy worn-out pair of brown loafers. He hoped to resemble someone who was down on his luck but still making an effort to look decent.

After storing all of his gear in the cab of the truck, Jack drove the mile to the driveway of Reverend Clyde's place and turned in. Since they had passed by an hour earlier, someone had put up a temporary sign with an arrow and the words "Church of the Swift Sword."

Jack joined a line of cars that extended from the treeline halfway back to the road. The car in front of him was an old Ford station wagon with Tennessee plates and a mattress, box springs, and several cardboard boxes tied to the roof. Inside the car, four adults and four children vied for space with stacks of clothing and more boxes. A boy of ten or so bared his teeth at Jack through the rear window and contorted his face in what might have been an imitation of a snarling cat. Or worse. Jack took a deep breath and admitted to himself that he was a little nervous about what lay on the other side of the trees ahead.

CHAPTER 16

First time here?" asked the beefy man who had stepped out of the stone guard house and leaned his head almost into Jack's truck.

Jack smelled the guard's breath and moved his head back a few inches from the porcine face that confronted him. The man's close-set, suspicious brown eyes darted about the interior of the cab and settled on Jack's Kelty rucksack.

"First time," said Jack.

"You got any firearms or alcohol in there?"

"No sir."

"Parking lot on the right," said the guard as he placed a small sign with the word "Visitor" behind the windshield wiper.

Twenty yards past the guard house, the treeline ended, exposing a scene that caused Jack to gasp. A massive fieldstone church loomed in the gathering darkness. Dim light escaped narrow slits of windows that ran vertically from near ground level to the top of the forty-foot walls. Four huge columns supported the roof of the broad, stone porch which led to the two twelve-foot wooden doors. At the front of the steeply inclined slate roof stood a bell tower on top of which rose a twenty-foot wooden cross. At the same moment that the bell began to ring solemnly, a car horn sounded behind Jack, who had stopped to take in the scene.

Jack pulled ahead and found a space in the large

gravel parking lot in front of a covered pavilion beside the church. Rows of aluminum picnic tables with attached benches covered the concrete floor of the pavilion. A crowd that Jack estimated at over two hundred moved busily about the floor carrying covered dishes and preparing place settings at the tables.

Jack got out of his truck and walked to the far left of the church. From that vantage, he saw four broad streets laid out in a semicircle fifty yards behind the church. Low-intensity street lamps lit the streets filled with small groups of people walking toward the church. Stone cottages lined three of these streets, which were the length of two city blocks. Each cottage had a small windmill on the roof and a solar collector atop a tracking arm in the yard. The street on Jack's far left had eight dormitory-type stone buildings. A group of khaki-clad men walked toward the church on one side of the street. On the other, small groups of three and four women wearing dark dresses walked together.

Behind the last houses, Jack could make out the shapes of several large barns and livestock pens. Behind those lay large fields of cultivated ground. In the failing light, Jack saw a tall wooden cross planted halfway up the mountain ridge that rose up from the edge of the distant fields. He stood looking at the cross until darkness obliterated it.

Jack walked back to the pavilion where a short, portly man in an ill-fitting blue suit met him.

"I'm Brother Olin and I don't believe I've seen you before. Is this your first visit with us? Brother . . . ?"

"Brother Jack. Yes sir, this is my first time. Mighty beautiful place y'all have here."

"Praise God and Reverend Clyde. It certainly is and we're proud to welcome you here. Let me show you to one of our special visitor's tables."

Jack followed Brother Olin to a group of tables in the center of the pavilion. Each table had a visitor's sign in the middle and a red and white checked tablecloth, unlike the surrounding tables, which were bare. Jack sat at the only one of the eight tables that was unfilled. Across from him sat the young boy who had made the face from the station wagon with Tennessee plates.

"Are you movin' here too?" the boy asked in a broad mountain accent.

Before Jack could answer, the man sitting on the boy's left did something under the table that made the boy wince.

"Hush up and mind your manners, boy," the man said with a glare.

"No harm done," Jack said, smiling at the boy.

The man turned to face Jack with a barely softened version of the glare that he had given the boy. The skin of his narrow face stretched tightly over the bones, accentuating prominent brown eyes glazed with an unhealthy luminosity. The scalp beneath his thinning brown hair was afflicted with eczema. As he stared at Jack, a gleaming white scale fell from his forelock and attached to the tip of his long, narrow nose. He crossed his eyes and stared at the end of his nose, then stuck out the lower lip of his tiny, pinched mouth and blew upward. Jack watched in amazement as the scale floated down and landed in the center of a red check on the tablecloth.

"Taught that boy better'n to go askin' questions of

strangers. I apologize."

"Like I said, no harm done. I was behind you at the guard house earlier and the boy and I saw each other then."

"Guess I'm a mite undone, mister. We just left Tennessee with everything we could carry and come here hopin' to make a stand with Reverend Clyde. Kinda puts a man out of sorts when he don't know what the future holds. I'm Lester Cade."

Jack reached across the table and shook the man's limp hand.

"I'm Jack. Pleased to meet you."

Jack was relieved when two teenaged girls arrived with cafeteria style trays heaped with steaming food. This special service seemed to have been reserved for visitors only. The other people served themselves at buffet tables laden with covered dishes prepared by members of the congregation.

Jack's tray contained baked turkey with corn bread stuffing, mashed potatoes, green beans, carrot and raisin salad, and a huge slab of pecan pie. Two large pitchers of iced tea were brought to each visitor's table in defiance of the cold night air that had settled upon the valley. The chill that Jack felt had no effect on the other people at his table. The Tennesseans had fallen upon their food like ravenous wolves. They ate with their heads bent over their plates, forkful after forkful of food flying from plates to mouths.

When Jack had finished eating the vegetables and the pie, he looked up to find the boy staring hungrily at the turkey on his tray. Before Jack could offer it to the boy, a serving girl whisked the tray from in front of him.

The boy's eyes followed the tray wistfully until the girl was out of sight.

Jack excused himself and rose from the table. On his way out of the pavilion, he stopped one of the serving girls and asked if she could point out Clint DuBois. The young girl gave him an odd look and told him that Clint wasn't around anymore.

Jack walked to the front of the church and looked up at the bell tower under the wooden cross. Four breast-high stone walls formed the lower part of the tower, giving it the fortified look of a gun tower. There appeared to be room for at least four men, one for each direction. A voice from close behind startled him.

"I hear you were inquiring after Clint DuBois."

Jack turned and faced the man whose approach he had not heard. He was tall and well built from what Jack could see in the dim light. Jack's shadow obscured the man's face.

"I was hoping to find out something about the survival school I read about a while back."

"Clint hasn't been here for over nine months. I'm Early VanZant. I took over security and the survival school after Clint left. So you're interested in survival, are you Mr. . . . ?"

Jack moved a step to his right in order to remove the shadow from Early VanZant's face. A pair of deep blue eyes peered inquisitively at Jack from a broad, square face that had a pug nose and a lantern jaw. A fleshy, feminine mouth sat incongruously between the feisty nose and the exaggerated jaw. The blond, almost platinum hair was cut in extremely short, military fashion.

The huge bell ringing the congregation to services drowned out Jack's answer.

"Catch me after the services," said Early VanZant as he walked toward the front steps.

As he watched VanZant stride toward the church, Jack pondered the fact that less than five minutes had elapsed between his questioning of the serving girl about Clint DuBois and the arrival of the head of security. He resolved to ask no further questions and moved toward the steps of the church.

When he joined the long line of people entering the massive double doors, Jack noticed that there were three distinct groups of people within the congregation: families consisting of husband, wife, and children; single young men between the ages of twenty and forty years of age; and elderly people comprising the khaki-clad men and blue-frocked ladies that Jack had seen promenading down the streets of the dormitories. Many of the elderly men had the leathery, deeply lined faces and wasted bodies of alcoholics. The young men had something of a military air about them, as if they were in mufti.

At the front door, Brother Olin greeted Jack.

"Brother Jack, kindly take a seat in the visitor's section all the way down front on the right."

A wide maroon-carpeted center aisle divided long rows of polished wooden pews and ended in front of the pulpit over one hundred and fifty feet away. The smell of wood polish mingled with the scent of freshly cleaned laundry, creating a wholesome bouquet absent any hint of perfume or aftershave. The rapidly filling church was unusually quiet—talk was at a whispered minimum and the dominant sound was the discreet swishing of fabric as people settled into the pews.

An usher gestured Jack to the center seat on the second row near the front of the church. Clean-cut young men filled the front row on either side exclusively. The pulpit was a large polished oak affair with waist-high wings that flared back from the main floor of the church. Directly behind the pulpit were two uncushioned high-backed oak chairs. Choir boxes lined the walls to the right and left of the pulpit.

The high, narrow windows set into the unadorned stone walls were flanked by metal shutters into which view-slits, or gun ports, had been cut. Jack's eyes followed the windows up to the ceiling where a series of huge wooden beams ran across the vast room. He estimated the peak of the ceiling above the beams to be sixty feet high. The austere building gave the impression of solid strength and the ability to withstand a siege. Jack shivered and wondered if body warmth was the only source of heat in the church.

The overhead lights came up when the red-robed choir began to file in from the back of the church. A tall, thin man in a well cut black suit entered behind the last choir member and strode to the pulpit. When he spoke, his rich baritone voice filled the church without benefit of microphone.

"Please rise and turn to page sixty-two in your hymnals."

Jack removed a hymnal from the rack attached to the pew in front of him and found the hymn HAIL! THOU ONCE DESPISED JESUS! At a sign from the music director, a piano hidden from Jack's view on the left of the pulpit began to play the introduction. When the congregation began to sing, the acoustical power of the place transported the upraised voices of hundreds into seeming thousands. He felt an emotional tug as he listened to the hymn for the first time since his early youth.

"Hail! Thou once despised Jesus! Hail Thou Galilean King! Thou didst suffer to release us; Thou didst free salvation bring. Hail, Thou agonizing Savior, Bearer of our sin and shame! By Thy merits we find favor; Life is given through Thy name."

Jack joined in on the second verse and sang along until the hymn ended. The silence that ensued was powerful and pregnant with anticipation. When the music director descended the steps and found a seat in the congregation, the house lights lowered. Then a tall, gaunt, white-haired and white-bearded man emerged from a door behind the pulpit and walked slowly to it. A heavy white robe hung loosely from his body, reaching the floor and covering his feet.

Upon reaching the pulpit, the man bowed his head for a long moment. When he had raised his head and gazed out over the congregation, Jack saw a look of hatred written there that he had not seen since the passing of the mad mullah from Iran. The pale blue eyes glowed under the massive brow. They roamed the congregation and finally came to rest on the visitor's section. When he spoke, the basso profundo voice resonated with power and authority.

"I am Clyde Causey, prophet of the Lord Jehovah, God of Moses and Father of Jesus Christ, upon whose spoken commandment I have raised up this Church and gathered this flock. I welcome you visitors tonight in His name. Your presence is a sign that you have been called to walk upon the path of righteousness. May you never stray."

Clyde Causey gripped the wings on either side of the pulpit, leaned forward, and gazed out upon the entire congregation.

"Last Sunday I went up to the prayer cave where I prayed and fasted until time to come down here tonight. During that time, God has spoken to me and unfolded His final plan. Even now He calls me back to the cave for the final purification which I must endure before I can stand here worthy to impart His plan to you. After this short service, you must go forth and alert all brethren that this Sunday is to be the glorious day.

"When God spoke to me and commanded me to raise up this church and assemble this flock, He told me this would be a church of great deeds. He has now revealed that our task is no less than the cleansing of America.

"With the exception of our white Christian ancestors who founded this great country, the history of this wretched world is primarily a story of rejection of Jesus Christ, the true Son of God.

"Christ's own people, the Jews, rejected and scorned Him. They remain stiff-necked and unrepentant even today. The message of our Father's only Son has been broadcast to the far corners of the earth for almost 2,000 years. To what effect, you ask?

"The Moslem nation has set the false prophet Mohammed above our dear Lord. The idolaters in the East have not cast away their abominable graven images. They persist in worshiping a multitude of petty gods or the lotus-eating Buddah.

"Even worse are the followers of the Vicar of Beelzebub in Rome, elected of man rather than God. These are lower even than the atheists, for they subvert the word of God in His own name.

"Yes, many are the enemies of God. And they shall meet their reckoning. Yet, I have not named the greatest enemy of all, THE ENEMY WITHIN. Among our own Christian race live many who have rejected their birthright. The power-mad politicians sell us out to increase their stature. In their greed, businessmen sell us out to our enemies. The dope dealers spread poison to our young people and lead them down the road of damnation. These offenders of our Lord have grown up in the bosom of our Lord's love and rejected Him.

"Therefore, the first act to be performed in the cleansing of America is the culling of this dross that dilutes us. Only after cleaning our own house will we be ready for the great task that awaits us. Only then shall we be ready to restore America to the status of an all-white Christian nation bent before the will of God.

"Before I leave you to undergo my final trial, let us pray together silently for ten minutes. Then, go forth for the remainder of the week and fill your hearts with prayer. Return here Sunday ready to receive the plan of action that we have waited upon so patiently.

"Now, let us pray."

At Reverend Clyde's last word, the lights faded out slowly until the church darkened totally. As an eerie silence descended on the place, Jack felt an energy manifest and build slowly. Somewhere in the back of the church, a person cried out. The building energy began to feel palpable and to swirl about Jack, seeking entrance into his innermost parts. He focused his energy between his eyebrows and began to meditate. As Jack opened himself to the increasingly powerful energy, the malevolence of it filled him with a hatred that constricted his heart. He plunged deeper and deeper into meditation, finally reaching the place where hatred cannot go.

Startled awake by the powerful chords of the piano, he found the lights turned up and the congregation on its feet around him. The floor was shaking under his feet and it took him a moment to realize that people were marching in place in their pews. As he rose to his feet, the voices of the congregation rose up powerfully in song.

"Mine eyes have seen the glory of the coming of the Lord; He is trampling out the vintage where the grapes of wrath are stored; He has loosed the fateful lightning of his terrible swift sword; His truth is marching on."

When Jack looked around the room, a bizarre sight greeted his eyes. Reverend Clyde had disappeared from the pulpit. Every fanatical eye in the house locked on the empty pulpit as the wide-open mouths shouted the words of the song. People swung their arms as they marched in place, creating a blur of motion throughout the church.

Jack left his pew and walked up the long center aisle at the beginning of the Glory Hallelujah chorus. Not an eye drifted in his direction.

When he finally got out of the church, Jack was gasping for breath and took in several deep lungfuls of the cold night air. The moon had risen over the mountain, bathing the valley in a clear, silver light. Across the fields, Jack saw a tall figure in a white robe striding toward the mountain. When the figure disappeared into the trees at the edge of the last field, Jack walked hurriedly to his truck and drove away.

CHAPTER 17

The narrow, deeply rutted, red clay and gravel road that led to Fate DeFoor's place wound through a series of fields and pastures before climbing steeply up the side of the mountain. Jack did not see the lights of the log cabin until he came suddenly into its yard after negotiating a hairpin curve. Instantly, a pack of baying black and tan hounds surrounded the truck. Fate walked out on the front porch and pulled a string below an exposed bulb. Then he waded into the pack of hounds, speaking to them as he walked to the truck.

"OK Boss, get back Lady, come here, settle down now, all of you, it's OK dogs."

"Don't worry none 'bout these here hounds, Jack. Their bark's a lot worse than their bite. Come on in this house."

Jack grabbed his sleeping bag and rucksack and stepped down into the milling pack of excited hounds.

"Evening, Fate. I'm gonna take you up on your offer, if it's still open."

"Sure it is. I was just takin' me a little dose of medicine. Come on in here and join me."

The cabin appeared ancient to Jack as he crossed the wooden plank porch. It was built of notched logs chinked in between with some sort of white plaster material. Inside, the long main room ran from the front to the back of the cabin. The wall on the right had three doors that opened directly into the main room. The wall on the left held a large open fireplace in its center. A roaring fire crackled, projecting a wall of heat and the homey fragrance of seasoned oak. Two wooden rockers sat on either side of a delicate cherry wood table in front of the fireplace. A quart Mason jar filled with crystal-clear liquid sat beside a small jelly glass on the table.

"Just drop your gear any ole where and take a seat, Jack. I swan boy, you look like you've done seen a haint. I got just the cure for that. Let me get you a glass."

Jack watched Fate walk to the kitchen area at the back of the main room and take a glass from a cabinet over the sink. When he returned, a devilish twinkle gleamed in his green eyes.

"Sit you down, boy," Fate said, gesturing to the rocker on the left of the fireplace.

Fate sat on Jack's right and carefully poured two fingers of moonshine into each jelly glass. He handed one glass to Jack and sat back in his rocker with the other.

"See if that don't cure what ails you."

The distinct smell of mellow corn wafted up to Jack's nose when he lifted the glass to his lips. He took a small sip and found the whiskey to be quite smooth with a hint of fire in the finish. After knocking the liquor back, he sat still and felt the trail of warmth move from his gullet to his stomach, then rebound upward through the region of his chest.

"That's as good as I've ever tasted, Fate."

"That there's the high wine, Jack. First run, uncut and stored in oak casks for five years. I have me a couple of nips every evenin'. Have for as long as I kin remember. Let's have us 'nother."

As he watched the old man pour another round Jack felt totally relaxed. He felt that he had known Fate DeFoor all of his life and that it was perfectly natural to be sitting here sharing a drink with him.

An easy silence settled between the men and held for a long while. They sipped their whiskey and rocked slowly in front of the fire. Finally, Fate drained his glass, placed his hands palms down on the rocker arms, and spoke as he stared into the fire.

"So what's your take on that bunch down the road?"

"I had a strange feeling during the service, Fate. It's hard to explain, but I felt like I was surrounded by some kind of evil presence. Never felt anything quite like that before. I guess that sounds kinda crazy."

"Not to me, it don't. I been livin' next to them devils for the better part of six years. Them people are rotten through and through. Straight to the core."

"Did you ever know of a man named Clint DuBois that used to be the head of security over there?"

Fate turned abruptly in his chair and cast blazing eyes upon Jack.

"Knew the son of a bitch and good riddance. Ran him off my land three times with my scatter gun. Haven't lost a dog since that sorry bastard cleared out."

"What happened to your dogs?"

"Found three of 'em with their throats cut. Right after they started tryin' to buy my land. Happened a couple of months apart. First time they was real nice. Offered me a good price. When I told 'em they could go to hell, they started showin' up on my property all dressed up in their play army clothes. Acted downright surly when I told 'em to get off. Then I found the first dog. After that, they made me another offer. A little bit lower than the first one. I told 'em again to go to hell and quit askin'. Found another dog. This time I went over there and laid into 'em good. Told that Reverend Clyde that if he didn't call his people off, me and him was gonna settle things personal.

Well sir, Reverend Clyde says to me that God wants my land and that one way or t'other he's a gonna get it. Then, he has them bully boys of his show me off the place. Next mornin', I found another dog."

"Damn, Fate, what did you do?"

"Well, first off I penned up my dogs. Then I sat me down and had me a good think. You see, son, there comes a time when each man has to look eternity in the eye and not blink. That time come for me quite a while back. I've outlived 'bout all the folks I care to 'cepting for that old bastard next door. It galls me to no end to think of him layin' hands on this land what's been in my family since the War Between the States. It come to me whilst I was thinkin' that they was atryin' to provoke me into somethin' in order to get me out of the way. Now, the only livin' relative I've got is the son of a second cousin. Hardly know the boy. Sure as shootin' he'd sell this place first off. So I decided to outlive ole Reverend Clyde. I figger when he's gone the whole kit 'n caboodle's gonna fall apart. Cut off the head and the body dies, if you know what I mean?

"So anyway, I penned up my dogs and waited. When that Clint fella cleared out first of last year, I turned the dogs out and haven't had a lick a trouble since. Only problem is, that ole devil next door don't seem to be slowin' down none."

"Well, Fate, it's just a feeling, but I don't think Reverend Clyde is long for this world."

"It's a fact that I'm not, so I hope you're right. I got somethin' to say to you Jack Lee 'n' I hope it don't offend you or give you the idea that I'm pryin' into your affairs. When you first showed up this afternoon, I thought you was the law. Then, after talkin' with you a while, I put that thought away. Now it seems to me that you've got somethin' agin' ole Reverend Clyde and if that's the case, well I'd say you and I's got common cause. So, I'm not askin' you to tell me nothin'. I'm just tellin' you that if you should need a little help from an old man what can hold a secret, all you got to do is ask. I don't normally cotton up to a man quick like, but I see you as a straight man. So I'll hush up now. Haven't spoke a piece that long in I can't remember when."

"I appreciate you saying that Fate. The truth is, everything is kinda muddy right now. If things clear up and we've got common cause, trusting you wouldn't be a problem."

A rustling somewhere in the back of the cabin startled Jack. When he looked quizzically at Fate the old man smiled.

"That's my pet coon, Bandit. He tends to get active this time of the evenin'. Wanna see him?"

"Sure."

Fate walked to the last door on the right at the back if the cabin. When he opened it and walked in, Jack heard the excited sounds of the coon bouncing around in a cage. The animal rode Fate's right shoulder back to the fireplace and peered warily at Jack from a vantage just below Fate's nose. After a few moments, the coon left Fate's shoulder and walked around the back of the rocker, where it sat and stared at Jack with bold black eyes.

"Takes him a while to get used to strangers. Next thing you know he'll be crawling all over you."

"How does he get along with the dogs?"

Fate reached over and poured a couple of small shots into the glasses.

"Well, we got us a little game. Now, I used to love nothin' better than to run my hounds all over these ridges and listen to 'em sing. Too old for that now, so I take old Bandit out and put him up in that big ole oak in the side yard. Drives the dogs plumb wild. Ole Bandit sits on a low limb and spits 'n hisses at 'em and I sit out there and take a few sips and take in the spectacle till the dogs are worn out. Course, it ain't the same as bein' in on the chase, but at my age, you take your fun where you kin find it."

"Must raise quite a racket?"

"Shoot, you can hear them hounds for miles around. I like to think it puts a burr in the saddle of them folks next door."

Bandit had slowly made his way to the floor and come to rest in front of Jack. He sat up on his haunches and licked his paws while staring steadily into Jack's face.

"Little beggar's tryin' to con you outa something to eat."

"What does he like?"

"Hell, he eats most anything. Got a special likin' for sweets. Never seen an animal with a sweet tooth like that."

Jack reached into the rucksack beside him and pulled out one of the huge Tree of Life peanut butter cookies. Bandit ran up his right leg, squatted on his knee and swatted at the cookie with both paws. When Jack opened the wrapper and held out a small piece of the cookie, Bandit reached with both paws and removed it delicately from his fingers.

"You've made a friend for life now, Jack."

When Bandit had finished the cookie, he jumped from Jack's knee to the top of the rucksack and started digging into it. Fate rose and neatly swung the coon up to his shoulder by the scruff of its neck.

"'Bout time I put the coon and myself away for the evenin', Jack. You can bring your stuff into this front room with you if you like."

Jack picked up his things and followed Fate into the frigid front room. When Fate pulled a string hanging from the ceiling, Jack saw in the dim light of the exposed bulb an old brass double bed covered with a stack of patchwork quilts, a chest of drawers with a large mirror, and a small bedside table with a porcelain water pitcher and a basin.

"I generally let the fire burn on out so you can leave the door open or shut to suit yourself. Won't make no difference. Bathroom's just next door. I'll be seein' you in the mornin'."

"Good night, Fate."

Jack pushed the door to, leaving a small crack, undressed, and climbed into bed. As soon as he stretched out between the flannel sheets, the bed swallowed him. After a moment of confusion, Jack realized that he was in an honest-to-goodness feather bed. He lay in the darkness waiting for his body heat to warm the bed and watched vagrant thoughts blow like tumbleweeds through his mind. Reverend Clyde's final plan from God. Why had his sermon made no mention of Negroes? Clint's absence. Fate's dead dogs. Darrell Day's dog. Was there a connection? The anonymous phone call to Courtney Fowler. Was it true? Smiley on the cross. Deborah. When the thought of Deborah O'Hara appeared, Jack held on to it and carried it with him into a dreamless sleep.

He awoke to an unfamiliar sound and lay still trying to identify it. The crack in the bedroom door admitted a pale light that accented the darkness of the room. Momentarily, the smell of percolating coffee helped Jack identify the sound.

Jack stretched out his right leg and immediately withdrew it. The bed was cold everywhere except the spots directly touched by his body. After building his courage for a long minute, Jack vaulted from the bed, gasping and shuddering in the cold. He dressed quickly and made a beeline for the fireplace.

After standing in front of the fire for half a minute, Jack turned his backside to it and gratefully felt the warmth move up his calves and the back of his thighs.

Fate walked from the kitchen, a grin on his face and a steaming cup in each hand. He handed a cup to Jack and eased in by the fire.

"Hope you like sugar in your coffee 'cause that's how it's served around here."

"Good morning, Fate. That's fine."

Jack sipped the strong black coffee and estimated that each swallow contained the equivalent caffeine of three No-Doz tablets.

"You come aflyin' outa that room like a streak, Jack. Hope it waddn't too cold for you."

"I'm a bit cold natured. Slept like a log, though. Woke up hungry as a bear, too."

"I imagine we can do somethin' 'bout that shortly. What you got in mind?"

"Well I've got a couple of cans of chili in my pack that I never got around to eating and some bread and cheese—think I might just go with that. There's plenty for both of us if you'd like to join me."

"Might just give it a try. What's your plan for the day, Jack Lee?"

"Well, I've got to head back down to Atlanta before noon. I was wondering, though, is there a place close by where I could get a good look at the lay of the Reverend's place?"

"That's easy enough. Right up the mountain here behind the house there's a finger of rock that sticks out of the side of the mountain and looks right down on the church. Don't take ten minutes to walk there."

After they had broken their fast on chili, toasted black bread, olives, and goat cheese, Fate pushed back from the kitchen table and shook his head.

"If someone had told me I'd be eating chili with no meat and all this other for breakfast this mornin' I'd a told 'em they was crazy. Fact is though, it was pretty danged good. Now, what say we take us a little hike?"

A blanket of heavy frost covered the ground and shimmered in the morning sun. Jack and Fate stood for a moment outside the back door, taking in the vast silence and watching their misty breaths curl from their mouths.

The sound of running feet broke the silence as the pack of hounds surrounded them and stood stiff-legged and trembling in the cold.

After a ten-minute walk up a steep trail, they came to a fifty-foot-long rock promontory that jutted from the side of the mountain and curved outward toward the church lands. They walked out to the end of the promontory and looked out upon a scene that took in all of Reverend Clyde's property. A flurry of human activity was visible around the livestock pens.

"Looks like they are agittin' ready to slaughter some hogs," Fate said.

"What are those dormitory buildings for? Who lives in them?"

"Well some of 'em's for the homeless men and some's for the homeless women and some's for the single men, them young bullies, militia or whatever 'n hell they call themselves. Word is ole Reverend Clyde rounds up these homeless folks, the ones with social security that is, and has 'em sign over their checks to the church. Mostly a bunch of old drunks and widder women, I think."

On their left, farther up the mountain, Jack saw clearly the wooden cross from the night before. It was planted in a small grassy terrace, behind which stood a formation of bare rock. Below a crack that ran down between two large boulders there appeared to be a head-high opening eight or ten feet wide.

"That there is Thigh Bone Cave," said Fate, who had followed Jack's gaze up the mountain.

"How big is it?"

"Goes back for a good ways, maybe thirty feet. Tall

enough to stand up in without havin' to bend over. There's a tiny little spring in the back. Got some mighty sweet water."

"I don't see any guards. Does Reverend Clyde stay up there all alone on these prayer fasts?"

"Just him and God. He don't allow anyone near that cave when he's talkin' to God. Guess he figures God'll protect his sorry ass."

"Where is that trail that comes down from the Pocket?"

"You're standing on part of it now. Starts out right behind that clearing I showed you up there and comes right down the side of the mountain. 'Bout even with that cross it makes a fork. Left fork heads toward the cave, right fork comes right on down this way."

Jack took a final look at the community spread out below him. Activity was picking up and people bustled purposely about their morning chores. The blades of the windmills turned lazily in the light morning breeze, and sunlight reflected from the solar panels. The sound of children's light laughter rose to Jack's ears, and he marveled that such a pastoral scene could be filled with such malice.

"Well, Fate, I guess it's time for me to push on."

"Reckon so. 'Bout time for me to get down there and open the store."

After making up the feather bed, Jack carried his gear out to the truck and started it. While the engine warmed up, he dug into his rucksack and found the last peanut butter cookie. When he looked up, Fate was standing beside the truck. Jack handed him the cookie with a smile.

"This is for Bandit."

"And this is for you, Jack Lee," said Fate, as he handed him a quart Mason jar filled with moonshine.

"Drink a toast to ole Fate DeFoor ever' once 'n while."

"Thanks for everything, Fate. It's been real."

"Come back 'n see me. You're welcome any time."

"May be sooner than you think."

Jack backed up and pointed the truck down the driveway. When he looked back toward the cabin, Fate threw his left arm high over his head and grinned a wrinkly grin. It's gonna be a sadder world when Fate DeFoor's breed dies out, Jack thought as he headed for the city.

CHAPTER 18

When Jack reached the intersection of I-75 and I-285 at noon, he exited to call the Thin Man. Thin answered on the first ring and spoke with a voice edged with excitement.

"I need to see you. How soon can you make it?"

"Thirty minutes?"

"The gate will be open."

Jack hung up the phone and drove to Thin's, prickled by a growing anticipation and the uncharacteristic excitement that he heard in Thin's voice.

When he parked the truck behind the house on West Paces, Jack found Lucy pruning bonsai plants on the patio. He wore an ankle length, orange and white floral patterned muumuu. The tiny pruning shears he held looked like a silver toothpick in his huge paw.

"Hi, Jack. He's waiting for you in the gazebo."

"Thanks, Lucy. Wonder what Paul Bunyan would think?"

Lucy threw back his huge blond head and laughed heartily in his high-pitched soprano voice.

"Oh Jack, you are SUCH a joker."

Jack walked to the large lattice-walled gazebo that faced a small stand of dogwoods and willow trees in the back of the sprawling yard. The Thin Man was sitting in a mahogany deck chair. He wore a pajama-like outfit of shiny black satin silk and woven Indian sandals. When he removed his sunglasses, the sunlight admitted by the latticework highlighted the yellowish cast of his light brown cat's eyes.

"Have a seat, Jack," Thin said, motioning to a deck chair on the other side of a gray, wrought iron table.

Jack sat in the sculpted wooden chair, which had a small brass marker with the words *SS Bremen* at its foot. Under the table, he noticed a small blue duffel bag.

"I had an interesting visit last night from a character with whom I rarely do business. This guy is an old Viet Vet who's primarily an arms dealer, but dabbles in herb, usually of the commercial variety. He brought me this to look at."

Thin reached under the table and handed the duffel bag to Jack. Jack unzipped the bag and found a half-filled garbage bag tied in a knot at the neck. When he untied the knot and opened the bag, a deep, winy aroma filled his nostrils. It was the unmistakable fragrance of Oakland Indica. He reached into the bag and pulled out a long, untrimmed limb. The flowers on the stem were damp to the touch. Even in the uncleaned and undercured state, the herb was unmistakably distinctive.

"Think there's any doubt?"

"None," said Thin. "I smoked it. That's Smiley's shit."

"How much is there?"

"One hundred and forty pounds. It was offered to me at fifteen hundred a pound, as is."

"And?"

"And I told the man that I would take it rough, but not wet. I told him to have his friend cure it for another day and have ten ready at noon tomorrow for me to look at. I set Saturday morning to buy the remainder. I wasn't sure when you were coming back, so I thought it best to string things out a little bit."

"That's fine as long as someone doesn't buy it out from under us."

"No problem. My guy called back this morning. The terms are acceptable."

"Did he by any chance mention his friend's name?"

"Well, when I expressed some concern over not knowing the source of the herb, my man said not to worry because his friend Clint was one straight-up dude. Does that mean anything to you?"

"It sure does, Thin. That is the guy who did Smiley. Now where do we go from here?"

"I've given that a great deal of thought. Whatever you do must be done before Saturday morning. I can't risk putting any of my people in harm's way. My guy is coming here to get the money for the ten at 11:30 tomorrow morning. He's supposed to meet his man, make the exchange, and bring me the herb. If all is well, we set a time and place Saturday morning for the rest."

"Then I need to be in place to follow your man out of here tomorrow morning."

"Exactly. You are on your own from that point on, Jack. Your only shot is to follow this Clint person after the exchange and hope he leads you to the stash. If he does, you've got almost twenty-four hours to do what-ever it is you plan to do."

"I'm going to have to cruise the road and wait for your man to leave here. What's he drive?"

"An old restored BMW 2002. Fire-engine red. You need to give him plenty of room. He's totally in the dark about all of this. I'll see that he leaves at 11:45. That's the best I can do."

"That's plenty, Thin. Thanks."

"No thanks necessary. When I said that you're on your own, I meant that I can't get directly involved. Anything short of that though, you are welcome to call. I'll do whatever I can."

"Well, I've got some getting ready to do. I'll be in touch."

The Thin Man turned his faraway eyes on Jack and held out his long, bony hand.

"Good luck, Jack. Watch your back."

"Always. Thanks again."

Jack took Thin's hand and held it for a moment. Some silent understanding passed between the men which they acknowledged with wry smiles. Then Jack turned and walked back to his truck.

Lucy met Jack beside the truck and placed his powerful hands on Jack's shoulders. His ice blue, Viking eyes held a look of concern.

"You be very careful out there, Jack Lee. We would hate to see anything happen to you."

Jack nodded affectionately at the gentle giant and slipped away from his grasp.

"Thanks, Lucy. See you soon."

At the end of the driveway, Jack stopped and deliberated whether to call Darrell Day. No, he thought, it's best to cut him out of the loop for now. No need for two of us to get shit on our shoes.

Jack took Moore's Mill Road out to I-285 and headed south. When he hit I-20, he headed west. An hour later, he pulled down Smiley's long driveway and parked in front of the small outbuilding that housed Smiley's workshop.

When Marge met him at the steps of the deck, Jack knew at a glance that she was having a hard time. The circles under her eyes had grown darker and she had lost weight. She fell into Jack's arms and buried her head in his shoulder. Jack held her close for a while, then led her into the house.

The bright silver urn on the mantle of the fireplace leapt out at Jack's eyes the moment they entered the living room. When Jack looked back at Marge, she nodded.

"Yesterday. He always said he wanted to be cremated. I was waiting for you before casting his ashes on the river."

Jack led Marge to the sofa and sat beside her.

"There is something I need to do first, Marge. I'll come back when it's finished."

"You know who killed Smiley?"

"I think so. Where are the kids?"

"They stayed in Atlanta with Smiley's parents after the service. I needed some time to be alone. I hope you don't mind, Jack."

"Mind what, Marge?"

"That I had the service without you. I just needed to get it over with. I'm sorry."

"Don't be. You did the right thing. Is there anything I can do?"

"Just what we talked about before. Find out why this happened. I need to know before I can get on with my life."

"I need to dig up the equipment. Smiley didn't

mention moving it, did he?"

"Not to me."

"I'll need the key to the workshop, too."

Marge walked into the kitchen and returned with a key on a loop of string.

"What's about to happen, Jack? Why do you need the equipment?"

"I don't know how this is going to play, Marge. It's probably best that we don't discuss it now. We'll have time for that later."

On his way to the workshop, Jack stopped at the truck and removed his rucksack. When he unlocked the workshop door, the smell of metal and oil mingled in his nose. He turned on the overhead light and emptied the contents of the rucksack onto the top of a large stainless steel table in the middle of the room. In short order, he found a five gallon can of mineral spirits, a clean three gallon aluminum bucket, a can of REM oil, and a stuffed sack filled with clean rags. He filled the aluminum bucket to within six inches of the top with mineral spirits. Then he grabbed the empty rucksack, removed a shovel from a toolrack on the left of the door and walked down to the river.

Jack walked north on the river bank for one hundred yards. When he came to a narrow slough, he turned left and followed it for fifty yards into the woods where it ended. Just beyond the end of the slough, a huge fallen walnut tree lay rotting. Jack walked from the uprooted base of the tree to its middle trunk and found an irregular stone. He placed his left heel against the stone, carefully measured ten toe-to-heel steps and started digging. Ten minutes later, he lifted a large, hard rubber bucket with an airtight snap-on lid from the moist earth.

Inside the bucket, Jack found two 9mm Mac 10 machine guns, packed in cosmoline, two Sionic sound suppressors, ten ammunition clips, two pairs of Army issue night vision goggles, and a small stockpile of 9mm ammunition.

After removing one Mac 10, one silencer, five ammo clips, one pair of night goggles, and half the ammunition, Jack reburied the bucket and covered the exposed earth with a layer of fallen leaves. The new weight of the rucksack dug into his back with each step and served notice that he was about to step over the line in a way that he had sworn never to do again. When he reached the riverbank, Jack stopped and listened to the gliding whisper of the Chattahoochee. What the hell am I doing, he asked himself and the river. From within himself, an ugly, sarcastic laugh arose. The river whispered unintelligibly and flowed on.

When he reached the end of the yard, Jack saw Marge sitting in front of the picture window, staring down at the river. He wondered briefly if there was something he could do for her, something that he had failed to think of. No, he thought, whatever solace is possible lies within her. Get on with it.

After soaking the weapon parts in mineral spirits, Jack cleaned and dried them thoroughly, then applied a light coat of REM oil. He assembled the ugly little piece, loaded the clips, and packed all of the hardware beneath some clothing in the rucksack. Then he cleaned up the workshop and returned to the house.

Marge had not moved from the window. She did

not turn when Jack entered the room.

"I left the key on the peg, Marge. The shop door's standing open—thought it could use airing out."

"I'll close it later. When will I hear from you, Jack?"

"I'm not sure. Soon, though. I'm headed out to my place now for the night unless you need anything."

"Just quiet. Come back safe."

When Jack locked his driveway gate behind him, he did not experience the usual feeling of peaceful relief. A sudden restlessness grabbed him, filling him with nervous energy that crawled on his skin. Although he was no stranger to the feeling, it was one that he had not felt for over three years, and he did not welcome it.

After unloading the truck and building a fire in the cabin, Jack changed into work clothes and walked outside to the woodpile. He began splitting three-foot sections of oak with a long-handled ax. Soon, he fell into a rhythm that he would pursue into the deep physical exhaustion that allows dreamless sleep.

Chapter 19

When Darrell Day's doorbell rang at 7:45 Thursday evening, Darrell was pacing the floors of his house in frustration. The three-day hard-on that he'd had for the world since Courtney's murder had gotten progressively worse since the death of his dog, and now Jack Lee's failure to contact him as scheduled. The result was a case of the emotional blue balls worse than he had ever known. His blood was so far up that he could feel the strain in his veins. He jerked his .45 from his shoulder rig and strode toward the front door hoping to find the ear surgeon but expecting to find Jack Lee whom he planned to read the riot act to.

Instead of Jack Lee, Darrell saw a tall, blond young man in a tan trenchcoat when he peered through the peep hole of his front door. Darrell moved the gun behind his back and opened the door with his left hand.

When Tommy Dalton reached into the left side of his coat, Darrell dropped the .45 to his right side. Dalton carefully pulled the lapel of his coat aside with the thumb and forefinger of his left hand and slowly reached for his ID with his right.

"Easy, Mr. Day," said Dalton as he withdrew a foldover leather wallet.

Darrell Day examined Dalton's credentials and handed the wallet back to him.

"What can I do for you, Dalton?"

"I'd like to ask you some questions. May I come in?"

Darrell stepped aside and motioned Dalton in, then closed the door. He did not ask Dalton to sit.

"Now what's on your mind, Dalton?"

"Courtney Fowler called your office at 1:05 Monday afternoon from her own office. The next call from that phone was at 1:13 P.M. to Manuel's Tavern. The bartender there confirms that you were there at that time and that you received a phone call from a lady, after which you left hurriedly. Now I stopped by Miss Fowler's about 1:10 to ask her a few questions about that crucifixion murder out in Carroll County. Just before we went to lunch, she said she had a call to make and asked me to wait in the lobby. I'd like to know why she called you? I'd like to know if that call had anything to do with the story on these ear chopper murders that she was working on before her death."

Darrell studied the man's face, feeling that he had seen him before. Whatever the case, he was an arrogant, self-satisfied cocker, and Darrell was already tired of him.

"She did call me at Manuel's on a totally unrelated matter. Now, is that all?"

Tommy Dalton looked down at Darrell with hard blue eyes.

"You don't remember me, do you Day?"

"Should I?"

"Ten years ago. The Hitchhiker Case. I was in charge of the investigation until you came waltzing in and pulled it out from under me. Fuckin' head fed. Well let me tell you something, Mr. ex-head-fed. You ain't jack-shit now, and if you withhold any information I'll jerk your license and bring you up on obstruction charges so fast your head'll swim. Do I make myself clear?"

Dalton's words jogged Darrell's memory and brought hot blood rushing to his temples. He stepped so close to Dalton that the agent felt his hot breath on his neck. When Darrell spoke, the words rasped out between his clenched teeth.

"You ever talk to me again like that I'll jerk your fresh mouth through your asshole."

Darrell's words penetrated special agent Tommy Dalton, producing a terror that turned his bowels to water and his mouth to cotton. He cut his panicked eyes down at Darrell and thought for a moment that the man was going to bite his neck. He took a step backward and tried to regain his composure. That effort failed miserably when he looked into Darrell's glowing black eyes. After a long uncomfortable moment, he ended all pretense of fearlessness and turned toward the door. When he had opened the door and stepped outside, Dalton turned as if to speak, then turned quickly and walked to his car.

Darrell closed the door and walked into the kitchen. As the adrenaline dissipated into his bloodstream, he felt a sudden letdown. He was pouring a double shot of Maker's Mark when the telephone rang. After tossing off the bourbon, he answered the phone and heard the neutral voice of the old colleague that he had queried about Clint DuBois.

"I got the information you wanted."

"What's your number? I'll step out and give you a call."

"No phones. I'm changing planes at Hartfield

tomorrow night. Meet me in the lounge of the main terminal building at 9:30."

Darrell hung up the phone and stood wondering what could be so sensitive about Clint DuBois that a face-to-face was required. Something ain't right here, he thought, as he resumed his pacing.

Chapter 20

At 11:45 Friday morning, on Jack's fifth drive-by of Thin's house, a fire-engine red BMW 2002 stopped at the end of Thin's driveway, then turned right and headed toward Peachtree Road. Jack pulled into the next driveway, turned around, and accelerated hard until he pulled to within sight of the red beamer. He followed it up Peachtree to Lenox Road, then into the parking lot of Lenox Square. Jack stopped just inside the lot and watched the driver of the BMW slowly cruise the packed rows of cars, looking from side to side as he drove. When he pulled the red car into an empty space beside a green Ford van in the middle of the lot, Jack cruised the row two back from them and found a space behind a Honda Civic that gave him a fairly clear view of the back of both vehicles.

A heavy-set bearded man emerged from the BMW and entered the passenger side of the van. After a minute or so, the van rocked slightly from side to side with movement. A curtain obscured the rear window of the van.

Ten minutes later the bearded man emerged from the sliding side door of the van carrying two oversized shopping bags. He walked casually to the rear of the BMW, opened the trunk, deposited the bags, slammed the lid, and got into the car. All of this was completed without so much as a look around or any sign of anxiety. The van remained in place for two minutes after the car had left, then backed out and headed toward Lenox Road. Jack waited until the van had passed his row, then followed.

The van turned left on Lenox, then right on Peachtree. At Peachtree-Dunwoody, the van turned left and headed north. Jack hung back a block or so and followed the van all the way out to Highway 400. When the van headed north on 400, Jack settled in a mile back and followed at 65 miles per hour. Twenty miles up the road, the van exited on state highway 120 and headed east. Just past the little town of Ocee, the van turned left onto a paved secondary road. Jack turned onto the road just in time to see the rear of the van disappear around a curve.

Jack raced for the curve, negotiated it and was confronted by a long empty straightaway. The van had disappeared. He slowed and searched right and left for a turnoff. Two miles down the road he came to a narrow, gravel driveway that angled back sharply to the left. At that point the paved road began to climb steeply. Jack drove a quarter of a mile and pulled off on a wide shoulder in the middle of a curve to the left. He got out, looked back toward the driveway and saw the green van parked outside a white frame farmhouse.

Fifty yards up the shoulder from where Jack stood, a wide power line cut through the woods and ran up a hill a couple of hundred yards behind the house. Jack walked up the power line and found a small turnaround that had been cleared for the use of the maintenance vehicles two hundred feet from the foot of the hill. He returned to the truck, drove down the power line to the turnaround and parked. When he walked back to the power line, Jack made sure that the truck was deep enough into the woods to be hidden from the road and started walking up the hill. The power line had been mowed recently. Barring problems on the line, Jack saw no reason for anyone to venture back into these woods.

When he reached the top of the hill, Jack dropped to one knee beside a large oak tree and took in the lay of the farmhouse. It stood on the far edge of a piece of bottom land that ran beside a creek flowing east-west a hundred yards behind the house, between Jack's hill and the house. A crescent-shaped driveway connected on both ends with the paved road. Jack had missed the first entrance because it entered the road at the end of the curve where he had momentarily lost the van. The road above the house occupied a bluff that dropped sharply, obscuring the house to the eyes of passersby.

As Jack started to rise, the back door of the house opened. A dark-haired man in jeans and a black T-shirt carried an aluminum trash can to a blackened fifty gallon drum and emptied the contents of the trash can into it. He leaned over the drum for a few seconds, then stood back. Momentarily, a plume of smoke rose from the drum. The man watched the fire for a minute before returning to the house.

Jack sat down beside the oak tree and studied the house. When his eyes came to rest on the power pole beside the house, a plan began to form in his mind. The fuse box just below the meter would have a throw switch. If he could get down there quietly and shut down the power, it might be possible to lure Clint DuBois outside where the night goggles should give Jack a strong advantage. The moon would rise at 8:30, so he needed to make his move no later than 8:00. Unless Clint left for some reason. If that happened, he could break into the house, remove the herb, and go back to wait for Clint to return.

As Jack sat thinking about the man inside the house, the idea of failure crept into his mind. Four people had met terrible fates at the hands of the man he planned to visit after dark. If he should become the fifth, no one would know about it. That was bad enough in itself. Even worse, Clint DuBois would get away with all of it. Jack thought again about calling Darrell Day and again rejected the idea. When an alternate plan popped into his head, he rose and walked back to the truck. Chances were, he figured, that Clint would not leave immediately after starting a fire.

Jack drove as quickly as possible back to the paved road and turned back toward Ocee and Highway 400. At several places along the way, he made note of the odometer reading.

When he reached Highway 400, Jack stopped and called the Thin Man from a pay phone. Thin answered on the fourth ring.

"It's me again."

"Ah, how was your drive?"

"Very productive. You said to call if I needed help."

"What do you have in mind?"

"I'd like to meet you somewhere. I'm out on 400. Could you make it out to the McDonald's at Holcomb Bridge Road and 400? What I have in mind won't take five minutes."

"I'm on my way. Give me twenty minutes."

Jack returned to the truck and got a pen and paper

from the glove compartment. He drew a detailed map to Clint DuBois's house on one side of the paper and wrote out directions to Darrell Day's home and his phone number on the other.

Thin's gray Jaguar was parked in the rear of the McDonald's lot when Jack arrived. Jack parked beside him and got out of the truck when Thin motioned him over to the Jag.

"So, all went well?"

"So far so good. I followed Clint to his house. I'll know more after dark."

"You're going in alone?"

"Yeah, that's why I wanted to see you. If you don't hear from me by 10:00, I'd like you to give this to a man named Darrell Day. Preferably by hand."

"Who is this guy?"

"You wouldn't believe it if I told you. He's got a stake in this and needs to know if something happens to me."

Thin studied both sides of the paper.

"No problem, Jack. By the way, things went smoothly this morning. The next meet is set for 11:00 tomorrow morning. Hopefully I'll hear from you before then."

"Hopefully."

When Jack reached the turnoff at the power line, he looked into his side mirror and saw the green van parked in the same place in front of the house. He drove down the power line in low and parked at the back of the turnaround. From the rucksack, he removed a heavy camouflage sweater, a black wool watch cap, and a pair of black, light-weight cotton gloves with raised metal beads on the grip side. After dressing, he slipped the rucksack on his back and walked up the hill.

Jack stopped beside a tall poplar at the top of the hill and stood quietly for awhile. When he was satisfied that Clint DuBois was not in the yard, he eased over to the large oak, withdrew a small tarp from the rucksack, and spread it on the ground beside the tree. He set the rucksack behind the tree, then sat Indian style on the tarp.

The mid-afternoon quiet, broken only infrequently by passing traffic, settled upon Jack, agitating an impatient part of him to action now that he had Clint DuBois in his sights. He set himself the task of watching his breath as it moved in and out. Slowly, his respiration waned to the point that long pauses occurred between breaths. After an hour or so, the sun dropped to the top of the treeline across the pasture behind the farmhouse. The trees cast long shadows across the pasture, forming intricate patterns as the sun descended steadily behind them. Jack watched as a huge circular web of shadows, connected to the four corners by a single strand, formed in the middle of the pasture. Suddenly, a hurtling form dropped from the sky and landed in the middle of the web. A huge red-tailed hawk rose slowly into the air, clutching a rabbit in its talons as its wings labored under the burden of the prize. A piercing cry of triumph shattered the silence as the hawk crossed the treeline.

Jack removed a small thermos and a Tupperware container from the rucksack. Might as well dine with the hawks, he thought, as he poured strong coffee and spread out two cheese sandwiches and some blue corn chips before him on the tarp.

He was eating the last chip when Clint DuBois came out the back door and emptied another load of trash for the fire. A cloud of ash and smoke rose from the drum. Jack focused a pair of field glasses on DuBois's face.

The eyes grabbed Jack's attention immediately. They burned amid the hollows and planes of his long, lean face. The heavy blue-black beard ran high up on his cheeks and halfway around the long neck. The long narrow nose and thin-lipped mouth gave the face a predatory look. The close-cropped black hair grew far down and formed a straight line across the slightly sloping brow.

DuBois's tall body was lean and corded with muscle. As he turned and walked back into the house, Jack picked up a hint of something simian in his movements. There was something familiar about the man's face that he couldn't put his finger on. Several minutes after he had stopped trying to remember what it was, the memory floated into his mind.

He had once read an article about men who had an extra male chromosome, a rare and somewhat aberrant occurrence. The bearers of this genetic imprint were often overly aggressive and tended toward extreme violence. A photograph of Richard Speck had been one of the several presented in the article. Clint DuBois's picture would have fit right in.

When the pasture had fallen completely into shadow, Jack removed the Mac 10, one clip, the silencer, and the night goggles from the rucksack. He took the remaining four clips from the main compartment and put two each into the top side pockets on either side and zipped them in so that a couple of inches of each clip stuck out from the top, within easy reach. Then he fitted the weapon with the silencer and popped a clip home with the palm of his left hand. After cleaning the lenses of the goggles, he stood and walked into the trees at the back of the hilltop. Ten minutes of stretching exercises restored full circulation to his cramped legs and feet. As the flowing blood moved behind his eardrums, it hummed an ancient tune, a tune that massaged Jack's adrenals with martial fingers. He returned to the tarp and sat Indian style watching his breath and listening to the flow of his blood as a chill settled in with the darkness.

When the luminous hands of Jack's watch read 7:45, he packed the tarp into the rucksack, slipped the rucksack onto his back and put on the night goggles. After allowing his eyes to adjust to the X-ray landscape, he started slowly down the hill. At the foot of the hill, something moved into view near the creek directly in front of him. A doe and two fawns lowered their heads in unison and drank from the creek. Several seconds later, a big buck with a large rack joined them. The buck lifted his head and tested the air with his nose before taking a drink. The deer stood silently for a few seconds after drinking, then moved to the far treeline.

When Jack reached the creek, the single light that had burned since darkness in the left front room of the house went out. Jack knelt in the cover of some low hedge bushes on the creekbank and waited. A door slammed, and then an engine turned over and cranked. The headlights of the van swept the pasture as it backed away from the house and pulled down the west end of the driveway. At the paved road, the van turned left and accelerated. Jack rose when the sound of the engine had ceased.

Jack stood stock still for a long moment, then jumped the small creek and closed the hundred yards between himself and the house with long quick strides. He threw the switch on the power box off, then walked around the house and checked for a security system. When he was satisfied that there was none, he climbed the back porch and knocked out the bottom right frame of glass on the top half of the Dutch door. After pulling back the slide on the Mac 10, he reached through the door with his left hand and found the turn knob for the dead bolt.

Jack found himself inside a long, spacious kitchen connected to the rest of the house by one door on the left that opened onto a wide hallway. Two doors stood open on the left side of the hall. The first room was bare save for a futon mattress covered by an unzipped sleeping bag, a Soloflex workout machine, and a giant poster of Adolph Hitler staring from the wall above the mantle of the fireplace. The front room on the left held only a recliner chair with a standing lamp to its left and a small table on its right and a thirteen inch Sony Trinitron perched atop a wooden crate. The closets in both rooms were empty.

Across the hall, Jack found a large bare living room and a bathroom. The closet and medicine cabinet of the bathroom were empty. Toothbrush, toothpaste, dental floss, disposable razor and shaving cream stood atop the sink. There was a dop kit on top of the toilet tank and a small plastic shampoo bottle beside a bar of soap on a tray hanging from the side of the large, claw-footed bathtub.

In the middle of the hall ceiling, Jack found a door with a cord hanging from it. When he pulled the cord, a set of folded attic stairs swung down behind the door. Jack pulled the stairs down and climbed to find an empty attic.

Puzzled, Jack returned to the kitchen. There, behind the open door on the wall on his left, he found another door. Upon opening it, he found a large walk-in pantry, empty except for a few cans of food. At the rear of the pantry there was another door. Jack opened it and saw a concrete stairway leading to a full basement. Halfway down the stairs, the smell of what he sought filled his nostrils.

The main room of the basement was bare except for a molded plastic chair that sat inside a large children's wading pool in the middle of the concrete floor. The area underneath the chair had been cut out exposing a metal drain.

On the left wall of the main room, there was a door beside which stood a knee-high metal faucet with an attached garden hose coiled at its base. Behind the door, Jack found a laundry room complete with washer and dryer. He also found twenty-three half-full black garbage bags stacked in a closet at the left end of the room. Mingled with the smell of marijuana, there was a foul odor, a smell of decay. When he looked to the far right end of the closet, Jack saw the source of the corrupt smell. On a knotted cord hanging from the clothing rod, eight human ears hung like the beads of a ghoul's necklace. Jack stared with a mixture of revulsion and fascination. Then he heard a soft whooshing sound in the air and the world went black.

Jack came to slowly through a swirl of nausea and vertigo. At the base of his neck, a deep pain throbbed at the place where his right shoulder joined the neck. When he tried to lift his head, a fresh wave of nausea swept over him and he vomited forcefully into his lap. The hot puke on his thighs informed him that his jeans had been removed. He took inventory and discovered that he was nude, except for his underwear. He was seated in a chair with his hands cuffed behind him and his legs tied to the legs of the chair. The total darkness of the room was disorienting, and the chilly air produced a violent fit of trembling. With effort, Jack drew several breaths and tried to clear his mind.

The door at the top of the stairs opened, throwing a shaft of light across the right half of Jack's body. Then, an overhead light came on and the door closed. Clint DuBois walked down the stairs carrying a gym bag in his right hand and the small table that had been beside the recliner chair in his left. A towel draped over his left shoulder.

DuBois placed the table three feet in front of Jack and set the gym bag on top of it. From the bag, he removed a long, thick cigar, a pearl handled straight razor, and a piece of soft yellow chamois leather filled with human dental impressions. With his back turned to Jack, DuBois produced a lighter from the right pocket of his jeans and lit the cigar. He turned and looked at Jack, a wreath of smoke framing his face. When he knelt at the edge of the wading pool and blew a long stream of smoke into Jack's face, Jack retched again.

Clint DuBois walked over to the faucet and turned it on. Then he picked up the hose and sprayed Jack down with a harsh spray of icy water. When all the vomit had been washed down the drain, DuBois turned off the water and came to kneel in front of Jack once again.

"Now, what is a Jackson Robert E. Lee?"

DuBois's voice was deep and calm. Jack looked into the man's dark eyes and tried to figure out how he knew his name. The dousing of cold water had hurried the onset of hypothermia and fogged his brain further.

"I went through your wallet, Lee. Now, who are you and how is it that you come to be here?"

"Fuck you," Jack muttered through chattering teeth.

DuBois rose swiftly and jerked Jack's head back by the hair, almost pulling out a handful by the roots. He ripped the towel off his left shoulder with his right hand and dried the top of Jack's chest. Then he puffed hard several times on the cigar and plunged it into Jack's chest just above the sternum.

Jack's body arched when the burning tip of the cigar hit his skin. He heard the sizzling sound of burning flesh and struggled not to scream. When the smell of burning hair and charred flesh reached his nostrils, a long roar of pain issued from his bowels and rose up through his mouth. The echo of that scream followed him as he slid down a long tunnel of darkness.

CHAPTER 21

At 8:45 Friday evening, Darrell Day switched on his answering machine and left his house for the airport. His frustration over Jack Lee's failure to contact him had been replaced by concern. His gut told him that something had gone awry and that Jack was in trouble. He had called Yeats Murphy and been told by a worried Yeats that he had heard nothing from Jack since Monday. The impending meeting with his old friend Jim Weston had added to the acid in his belly. Tricky Jim would not have demanded a face-to-face meeting unless there was a serious reason.

As he drove south to Hartsfield, Darrell examined his mixed emotions concerning Jim Weston. They had gone through the Academy together many years back and had been friendly, if not exactly friends. They had both been assigned to the Washington, D.C., area as shavetails. Early on, Jim had shown an ability to shit any shitter, quit any quitter, or con any con. He had cut his teeth on deep cover domestic stings and then moved up to the level where the distinction between domestic and international and one intelligence agency and another blurs and vanishes into a shadowy world of unacknowledged cooperation. Darrell had moved into the more pedestrian role of the field agent. After Darrell's transfer from the D.C. area, the two men had kept in touch in a scattered kind of way, meeting occasionally for drinks when Darrell was back in town for this meeting or that at headquarters. Jim Weston was capable of great charm and Darrell liked him personally. To a point. There was something elusive, less than solid, that had prevented Darrell from ever trusting him completely.

Darrell parked in hourly parking and walked to the bustling terminal. People of every color and nationality scurried about with dazed looks on their faces. When he entered through the sliding glass doors, a queasy feeling rumbled through his guts, a peculiar sensation that would have told him he was in an airport even if he had been blindfolded. He walked by the ticket counters and made for the sprawling lounge in the center of the building. Jim Weston rose from a corner table near the lounge entrance when Darrell was twenty feet away.

Weston wore a rumpled brown tweed sport coat with suede elbow patches, over a deep gold V-neck cashmere sweater and a white shirt open at the collar. His slightly baggy, fully-pleated brown slacks ended in full cuffs just above lace-up suede Hush Puppies. Darrell knew that beneath the professorial rags lay a superbly conditioned body that would be the envy of many men half Jim's age.

Only the fine lines about the friendly blue eyes and the downward tug at each corner of the large, full mouth belied the impression of youth that Jim Weston's face gave at first glance. The tousled mop of sandy hair topped a pleasantly rounded face, thrown out of symmetry by a long, extremely narrow nose.

Darrell took Jim Weston's extended hand and felt the firm, sure grip that he remembered from the earlier hand of youth.

"Good to see you, Darrell. Thanks for coming."

"You too, Jim. When I asked the favor, I never expected to see you in person."

"How about a drink?"

The men sat and looked at each other, each aware of the tension that made this more than a casual drink. Jim raised his hand and caught the attention of the attractive black waitress at the end of the bar. When she arrived, Jim ordered a Campari and soda, and Darrell asked for a double Maker's Mark on the rocks. After she left the table, Darrell turned to Jim and smiled a tight-lipped smile.

"Not being unfriendly or anything, Jim, but I've got a situation on my hands. One drink's gonna be about it."

"Situation where people are losing ears?"

The question hit Darrell like a crisp slap in the face. Before he could answer, the girl returned with their drinks. Darrell drank off half of his drink and leaned over the table.

"What the fuck's going on, Jim?"

Weston took a sip of his Campari and leaned over eyeball to eyeball with Darrell.

"Some people got mighty upset when I made that inquiry about Clint DuBois for you. These murders down here have been front page news all week nation-wide. Am I right in assuming that your interest in DuBois is related?"

"Maybe. What did you find out about him?"

"This is strictly on the Q.T. I might need a little something in return, too. This is a rather sticky wicket, Darrell."

"I can't promise anything."

"Is this something personal?"

"Very."

"OK, no promises up front. Hear me out and we'll take it from there. In the middle of Clint DuBois's third tour, the Special Forces tour, he got R and R and chose to stay in country. The best they could figure out later, he loaded up on supplies and went into the bush on a personal hunting trip."

"Hunting?"

"VC hunting. He didn't return. Three months later, some LURPS found him wandering half naked through a rice paddy in the upper Mekong Delta, wearing a necklace of human ears that hung down almost to his knees. Seventy-two pairs of ears to be exact. He was babbling out of his mind and had a raging malarial fever. When the LURPS got him back, he was stabilized in a field hospital and shipped directly stateside. After eighteen months of intensive psychotherapy, he was deemed fit to return to society. That could prove to be a very embarrassing error in judgment if DuBois is responsible for these murders. You know where this is leading."

"The government doesn't want Clint DuBois coming up for trial on something like this."

"One way or another. Preferably another."

"Meaning?"

"Meaning that it might be better for everyone if Clint DuBois disappeared. If he's the one. Are you sure that he is?"

"Not one hundred percent."

"How about the local boys? What have they come up with?"

"Zip, from what I can tell."

Jim Weston reached inside his coat and removed a small card from his shirt pocket. He studied it briefly, then placed it on the table in front of Darrell.

"There's a team in place in Atlanta right now. If you locate DuBois, dead or alive, call that number. They'll pick him up and sanitize the location, no questions asked. Frankly, Darrell, we don't think there is too much doubt about this guy."

"I'll make you a deal, Jim. You don't put anybody on me, leave me with a free hand, and I'll give you DuBois. One way or the other."

"You sound pretty sure, Darrell."

"Just a feeling."

Darrell rose and shook Jim Weston's hand. When Weston tried to release his hand, Darrell held on to it tightly. Weston met his hard gaze with questioning eyes.

"No tricks, Jim. I don't think I could take that."

When Weston nodded solemnly, Darrell released his hand and walked out of the lounge. He resisted the urge to run until he had cleared the sliding glass doors. Once outside the building, he broke into a trot and made directly for his car.

*　*　*

At 10:35, Darrell pulled into his driveway and found a Jaguar sedan parked outside his garage, with smoke curling from the exhaust pipe. A man's head was visible through the rear window.

Darrell pulled halfway up beside the car, placing the tip of his right front fender three inches from the door handle on the driver's side of the Jaguar. The driver of the Jag turned his head toward Darrell, allowing him a shadowy view of a long, narrow face with strange eyes that cast a yellowish glint into the night.

Darrell opened his door and stepped cautiously from the car, keeping his head below the roof line and shielding his body with the door and the body of the car. As he moved his right hand toward the .45 under his left armpit, a pair of massive arms closed around him like a straightjacket. A chin settled into the crown of his head and a soprano voice spoke soothingly to him.

"We're friends of Jack Lee, Mr. Day. I'm going to let go of you now."

As soon as he was released, Darrell spun around and saw a blond giant towering over him.

"Who the hell are you?"

"I'm Lucy."

"And I'm Thin," said the wraith-like figure that had materialized at Darrell's right elbow.

Darrell looked incredulously from one man to the other and wondered if his eyes were playing tricks on him in the weak light of the fixture over the garage door.

"You say you're friends of Jack? Where the hell is he?"

The Thin Man handed Darrell a folded piece of paper.

"Jack said to give you this if we had not heard from him by 10:00. He never called."

Darrell leaned inside his car and studied the paper under the dome light. When the implication of what he read hit him, adrenaline flooded his bloodstream. He leaped behind the wheel of his car and cranked up, rolling down his window as he did so.

"Thanks," Darrell said to the odd couple standing beside the car.

"Have Jack call me," said the Thin Man.

Darrell nodded and gunned the Chrysler down the driveway, cussing Jack Lee and hoping against hope as he drove.

CHAPTER 22

A distant chattering sound called Jack Lee back to consciousness. The sound intensified and moved closer as he drifted upward through hazy depths toward full awareness. Finally, he realized that he was listening to the sound of his own teeth clacking violently. He forced his jaws shut and opened his eyes to total blackness. A foul odor rose to his nose from beneath him, informing him that he had shit himself.

Humiliation mingled with the helpless rage that lay cold and useless in the pit of his guts. Despair settled into his bones, and he knew with certainty that he was going to die in this place. That knowledge sparked a fear that burned into recesses of memory long guarded by doors that locked in his deepest fears and secrets. Painful emotions released as the doors burned one by one. When the last door had burned, Jack stood revealed to himself in all his flawed humanity. Seeing himself clearly, for the first time, he accepted his own death and fell still. In that clear, peaceful moment of acceptance, Jack realized that he was not alone. He felt the presence of Clint DuBois in the dark room. A question arose suddenly in him and escaped his lips before he was aware that he would ask it.

"Why did you crucify him, Clint?"

Jack heard a soft sound in the direction of the stairs. The light came on, revealing Clint DuBois at the head of the stairway. When he descended and knelt in front of Jack, Jack was astonished by the change in the man's face. The hard features had softened into a look of rapture. The dark eyes glowed with an unholy reverence that bespoke some inner exaltation. Jack saw something almost childlike in the creature that he had come to think of as less than human.

"That was Reverend Clyde's idea. Why?"

"I'd like to understand that."

A look of disgust swept over Clint's face.

"You stink. Let me wash you off first."

Clint turned on the faucet and directed an icy stream of water between Jack's thighs and the bottom of the chair. Jack raised himself off the chair as far as possible and shuddered as the freezing water numbed his lower body. Clint looked almost solicitous as he performed the task, as if he were doing Jack a kindness.

After turning off the water and coiling the hose at the base of the faucet, Clint returned and knelt in front of Jack on one knee. His arms were crossed on top of his raised left knee, allowing Jack a glance at the watch on his left wrist. It was 10:40.

"Your time's up. You know that, don't you?"

Jack nodded.

"I need to know how you found me. That was you in the blue truck this afternoon, wasn't it?"

Jack nodded again.

"How you die depends on what you tell me. If you're straight with me, I'll make it quick. If not, well, you'll still tell me. It's up to you. I'll enjoy it either way."

"Tell me why you did Smiley, and I'll tell you what you want to know."

"You're in no position to bargain, but I guess it

won't hurt to tell you what you want to know. It won't do you any good where you're going. You jerk me around, though, I'll make you sorry. You understand?"

Jack nodded.

"Well Reverend Clyde's this crazy old fart who thinks he's gonna get America back for the white people. He's got this master plan and the first step is to clean up the white race. So Reverend Clyde hit on the idea of crucifying drug dealers, liberal politicians, left-wing media people and the like. Kinda scare the white folks into righteousness. Get 'em back on the path. Well Reverend Clyde thinks I'm just the man for the job. Then this fucked up little helicopter pilot falls into our hands. Flies a pot chopper for the state. This Smiley fellow's field just happened to be the first one big enough to fit the bill. Friend of yours, was he?"

Jack nodded. Clint DuBois had risen and begun pacing in front of Jack as he spoke. Each mention of Reverend Clyde had been spoken with undisguised disdain.

"You don't seem to buy into Reverend Clyde's program, Clint."

Clint jerked his head around and faced Jack. The softness had fled his face, replaced by a lip-curled look of malice.

"I'm crazy but I'm not that crazy. Only reason I ever signed up with that insane old son of a bitch is 'cause he's freighted down with money, and I thought I could get my hands on some of it. That and the blood-work. Any fool could see there'd be bloodwork around the crazy old coot. That's the two things I care about in this world, boy. Bloodwork and money. This little pilot fell into my lap; well, I saw my chance and took it. That pot back there in the closet's my ticket. Soon as I tie up a few loose ends, I'm outa here. Brazil for me, boy. Those big landowners down there are hiring men with my special talents. Ain't no law to speak of and lots of bloodwork."

Clint walked over to the table and picked up the cigar.

"Now it's time for you to tell me how you got to me," Clint said as he lit the cigar and stoked it with several long puffs.

Jack looked into Clint's black eyes and saw nothing but business there. The conversation was over.

"Just lucky I guess," Jack said sarcastically.

Clint leaped toward Jack and jerked his head back savagely by the hair with his left hand. He brought the cigar close enough to the skin to burn without touching and held it there beside the deep burn above Jack's sternum. Then he lowered his face to within an inch of Jack's and pressed the cigar into the skin lightly.

Jack gritted his teeth and struggled not to cry out. A cold sweat popped out on his forehead and was warmed by the hot breath that came from Clint in heavy pants. Jack looked at Clint's face and saw the slack look of arousal there. When Clint jammed the cigar into his chest, Jack screamed and began to fade out. Clint withdrew the cigar and stood over him, breathing in heavy spasms.

"You don't know what you're dealing with here, boy. You better talk to me or I'm gonna feed you your ears."

Jack whispered for Clint to lean over. When he did,

Jack spit hard onto his face. Clint jerked back and took a step away. The bulge in the crotch of his jeans confirmed what the slack look on his face had suggested. Clint saw where Jack's look was directed and glared at him with hate-filled eyes.

"You're a sick sack of shit DuBois," Jack rasped through clenched teeth.

Blood rushed into Clint's contorted face, turning it into a demonic purple mask. He picked up the pearl handled straight razor from the table and opened it with a flick of his wrist. Two quick strides brought him beside Jack. He grabbed a handful of Jack's hair and twisted his head to the left, exposing the right ear to the blade. Jack stared straight ahead at the bottom of the stairs and waited.

"Now you gonna talk to me, boy?"

As Jack searched his blank mind for something to say that might forestall the loss of his ear, a black-tasseled loafer touched the bottom step in front of him. The sharp blade touched the skin below the earlobe and began to move upward.

"OK, OK, OK," Jack screamed, dragging out the words as long as possible.

As he screamed, the black shoes moved swiftly across the floor. The blade left Jack's ear. Then there was the unmistakable metallic click of a weapon being cocked. Jack felt the hand release his hair and looked up to see Darrell Day pressing the snout of his .45 into Clint DuBois's neck.

"Drop it and step back very slow. Give me a reason and I'll do you right now," said Darrell in a low I-mean-business voice.

Clint dropped the razor and stepped slowly out of the wading pool.

"On the floor. Face down. Slow and easy."

Darrell kept the gun pressed into Clint's neck all the way to the floor.

"Put your hands behind your back," Darrell said as he pulled a set of handcuffs from the pocket of his sport coat.

Darrell cuffed Clint and stood away to look at Jack. Darrell shook his large head slowly from side to side, a look of relieved exasperation on his worn face.

"You're a real piece of work, Rhett."

Jack felt a witty repartee die on his tongue.

"Untie me, Darrell," he said quietly.

Darrell stepped into the wading pool and untied Jack's legs, then helped him to stand. Jack almost fell when the blood rushed into his numb feet and ankles. Darrell rummaged in the gym bag on the table for the metal key to unlock Jack's handcuffs. Jack massaged his wrists and stamped his feet on the cold concrete floor until his circulation was fully restored. Then they both looked at Clint DuBois on the floor and, without a word between them, lifted him into the chair, and tied his ankles to its legs. Clint's face darkened when he saw Darrell.

"You! What the fuck are you doing here?" asked Clint, a look of bewilderment slowly passing over his face.

"Shut your mouth," Darrell said.

Darrell picked up the chamois cloth and studied the tooth marks on it. When his puzzlement changed slowly to comprehension, he grabbed Clint by the cheeks, with the thumb and forefinger of his right hand, forced his jaws open and stuffed the chamois into his mouth.

Jack removed his fouled underwear and washed himself off with the hose. He found his clothes on the floor of the laundry room and dressed. As the sweater dug into the burns on his chest, he cursed under his breath.

"There any doubt about this guy?" Darrell asked from the main room.

"Come in here a minute. Something I want to show you."

Jack opened the closet door, switched on the light and motioned Darrell into the closet. Darrell saw the necklace of ears and lowered his head. A tremor shook his shoulders and a partly repressed sound escaped his mouth. When he looked up at Jack, murder gleamed in his eyes.

"Fucking animal."

"What are we going to do with him?" Jack asked.

Darrell filled him in on his meeting with Jim Weston.

"What exactly does that mean? 'Sanitize the location'?"

"It means they'll professionally erase all signs of his presence here. A complete wipe job."

"Then what happens to DuBois?" Jack asked.

"They can bury him or cremate him 'cause that animal ain't leaving here alive."

"Then that only leaves one question. Gotta coin?"

Darrell removed the black leather glove from his right hand and fished a quarter from his pants.

"Call it," he said, as he flipped the coin.

"Tails."

Darrell caught the coin with his gloved left hand and covered it with his right. He stood motionless for a moment, then uncovered the coin. It was tails.

"Damn," Darrell swore. "You up to this?"

"Absolutely."

"Anything you want me to do?"

"Just leave. I'll call you at home when it's finished."

"Last time you said that I sat around for two days. What time will I hear from you?"

"By the time I finish with him it's going to be too late to be driving around with that shit in the back of my truck," Jack said with a nod toward the closet. "Think I'll haul the herb up to the power line where I'm parked and wait for the first light. I'll call you from the highway."

"Call from the first phone you see," Darrell said emphatically. "Sooner I get these guys here to clean up the better."

They walked back into the main room and stopped in front of Clint DuBois. Darrell stared at him for a long minute.

"Burn in hell, asshole," Darrell said.

Clint smirked as best he could with a mouthful of leather.

Darrell turned and walked toward the steps. When he was halfway up, he turned and looked back, as if to speak. Then he turned and left silently.

Jack put on his light cotton gloves and pulled the chamois from Clint's mouth. He walked to the table and picked up the straight razor.

With a flick of the wrist, he opened the razor and admired the gleaming, honed edge under the light.

"What do you have to say now, Mr. DuBois?"

"You don't have the balls," Clint said with derision.

Jack turned to face Clint. When Clint saw the look on his face, he leaned as far back as possible in the chair, eyes wide and starting from his head. His lips mouthed a silent "no" as Jack moved toward him.

CHAPTER 23

First light, bleak and gray, came grudgingly, exposing a thin wet mist dancing before the strong north wind that had risen before the dawn. Jack Lee, cold and exhausted, started awake from a fitful doze and cranked the truck. As the engine warmed up, he struggled to bring his senses into focus, then drove slowly down the power line. At the paved road, he turned right and turned on his lights. The trauma of the previous night had combined with the lack of sleep to produce a strange giddiness, an uneasy lightness of head and body. His eyes played tricks on him in the half-light and the mist.

When he reached Highway 400, Jack stopped at a pay phone and made two calls. Darrell Day answered anxiously on the first ring.

"Hello."

"You can make that call now."

"You OK?"

"Yeah. Sort of."

"Yeats Murphy called. Wants you to call him."

"I'll call him tomorrow. See you tomorrow, too."

"You're going up there?" Darrell asked, after a long pause.

"Yeah."

"Maybe you ought to give it up."

"Maybe. See you tomorrow."

The Thin Man answered sleepily on the fifth ring.

"That you, Jack?"

"What's left of me. I need to stop by."

"You have your friend with you?"

"Regular bundle of joy."

"I'll open the gate. Drive on back into the garage."

"Thirty minutes."

Jack drove south toward the city as if in a dream. A bizarre urge to laugh came over him, an urge fraught with hysteria. He resisted the laughter for fear that, once started, there would be no end to it.

"You watching all of this, Smiley?" he asked out loud.

Jack felt a wave of relief when he passed through the Thin Man's gate. He drove back to the four car garage and pulled into the open door on the far right. The door began to descend as soon as he cleared it.

The Thin Man was sitting on the fender of his Jaguar, a cup of coffee in his hand. Beside him sat a silver thermos and a cup.

"Jesus, Jack! You don't look too good," he said as he poured coffee into a cup and handed it to Jack.

"Kind of you to notice, Thin."

"You are welcome to crash out in the guest room for a while."

"Thanks, but I'm feeling a real need to sleep in my own bed. As soon as we unload this shit, I'm headed for the ridge."

"Bad scene, huh?"

"Ugly. I'll tell you about it one day. If it's OK, I'm going to let you take care of weighing this shit up."

"That's fine. I've got a buyer set to take it at noon. When shall I hear from you next?"

"Hopefully tomorrow morning. I've got one more thing to do. If you don't hear from me for some reason, get the money to Smiley's wife."

"No problem. Let's stack these bags over in this corner for now and get you on the road."

They removed the plastic bags from the bed of the pickup and counted them before stacking them in the back corner of the garage. Thin opened one bag and nodded his head approvingly.

"Shouldn't be any problem. Be careful out there, Jack."

"Mañana, Thin. Thanks for the coffee."

A powerful, gusting north wind buffeted the truck as Jack drove west on Interstate 20. Several of the windy broadsides almost blew him into the next lane. A weak sun had risen in a clear, pale blue sky, adding light but little warmth to the day.

In Douglasville, he exited and stopped at the Home Depot. The icy wind drove people quickly from their cars to the warmth of the store. The temperature must have dropped ten degrees since sunrise.

Inside the store, Jack found a two pound, short-handled sledge hammer and some heavy six-inch nails. He overheard a conversation in the check-out line and learned that an Alberta Clipper was bearing down on the South, bringing unseasonal frigid air that threatened to drop below freezing by morning.

When Jack returned to the truck, the ripe smell of decay had filled the cab. He sat nonplussed for a long moment before remembering the sack of ears beneath the seat. When he leaned down to move them to the other side of the truck, bile rose in his throat. He sat upright and held onto the steering wheel until the nausea passed.

During the forty mile ride home, Jack left his window partly open. The clean cold air neutralized the smell of corruption and helped him keep his tired eyes open. When he finally reached the ridge, he parked in front of his gate and slumped back in his seat. The temptation to stretch out on the seat and sleep was strong. With effort, he forced himself out into the cold and opened the gate.

The inside of the cabin felt colder than outdoors. Jack threw some logs into the fireplace and lit a few sticks of fat lighter under them. The sharp fragrance of the resinous pine lighter bit his nostrils as it burst into flame. As he warmed his hands over the fire, the burns on his chest began to itch and sting, like the bite of the fire ant. The skin around the wounds began to tighten and draw in rhythmic contractions. When he took off the sweater, the fabric pulled out of the skin.

The wounds stared back at him from the bathroom mirror like angry cancerous eyes. The eyes in his head looked even worse, so wild and desperate that Jack was forced to look away.

He bathed the burns with peroxide, then dried them and applied an antiseptic. With tired, awkward fingers he fashioned a large bandage that covered both wounds, then took a soft flannel shirt from the doorknob.

He dragged out his goose down mummy bag from the bedroom closet, grabbed the clock from the bedstand, and returned to the living room. After drawing the blinds, he lay on the sofa and reached for the clock on the table. It was 10:00 A.M. He set the alarm for 6:00 and fell back into the pillows. His body heat soon transformed the mummy bag into a warm cocoon in which he floated, womblike and secure for a few conscious seconds. Then he fell into the watery depths of oblivion.

Eight hours later, his body resisted the wake-up call of the shrill alarm. His eyelids felt glued over grit-filled eyes and his muscles felt atrophied on his bones. A sweet whisper in his head urged him to turn off the alarm and return to the waiting arms of sleep. Finally, the insistent alarm jangled him off the sofa.

After three cups of strong coffee, coherency returned to Jack's mind, accompanied by a strengthened resolve to see through the awful plan that had emerged there full-blown and unbidden. He cooked a large breakfast of scrambled eggs, grits, and whole wheat toast and washed it down with two glasses of milk. He wasn't aware of the extent of his hunger until the first bite triggered wolfish gulps.

Replenished, he went into the bedroom and dug out heavy wool socks and polypropylene long underwear from the chest of drawers. Over these, he put on jeans, a heavy wool shirt, a down vest, and insulated hiking boots with vibram soles. From the rucksack, he removed the wool watch cap and light-cotton gloves which he exchanged for a pair of fleece-lined heavy leather ones.

Outside a steady twenty-mile-per-hour north wind moaned in the treetops like some ancient squaw turned out by her tribe to die in the night. Overhead the stars blazed fiercely in the cloudless firmament.

Jack walked briskly to the toolshed, opened the

door, and turned on the light. In the right rear corner, he found a folding camp shovel and two screw-on extensions that lengthened the metal handle to full size when attached. He closed the shed and walked back to the cabin, grabbing the ax from the woodpile as he went.

The thermometer beside the back door read twenty-five degrees. Jack entered the relative warmth of the cabin and set about packing. He emptied the rucksack on the coffee table in front of the fireplace and fetched a stack of hand towels from the bathroom. In the left compartment of the rucksack, he placed the sledge hammer, nails, and handle extensions for the shovel, putting towels between each metal object to muffle metal on metal noise. In the right compartment, he repacked the Mac 10, the ammo clips, and the night goggles, separating them with towels and securing them against movement. From a roll of thin nylon cord, he cut several three-foot lengths, which he stowed in a side pocket. Finally, he slipped the handle of the shovel through a loop on the back flap of the rucksack and secured the shovel head with a bungee strap.

After packing a change of clothes in a small duffel bag, he stood quietly for a moment and took inventory. Then he placed the screen in front of the fireplace and walked out the door.

CHAPTER 24

At 9:45, Jack Lee pulled into Fate DeFoor's front yard. The truck was immediately surrounded by the pack of aroused hounds who milled like ghostly shadows in the light of the full moon. Fate opened the front door and stepped onto the front porch.

"Is that you, Jack Lee?"

Jack stepped out of the truck and walked to the porch, escorted by the excited dogs.

"It's me, Fate. Sorry to slip up on you so late."

"Glad to see you. Step on in out of the cold, boy."

"Haven't got time, Fate. Wanted to ask you a favor."

Fate reached up and pulled the string below the exposed bulb on the porch ceiling. He studied Jack's face for a moment, then nodded.

"Ask away, Jack."

"Well, I was thinking it might be a good night to put ole Bandit up in that oak tree."

"Might be at that. I ain't seen a moon like that 'un in some time."

"Maybe you could give me an hour start?"

"Wouldn't be no trouble a'tall. How long you think ole Bandit might oughter tease these boys?"

"Till their lungs give out, Fate."

Fate looked up at Jack with appraising eyes and rubbed the silver stubble on his chin.

"When will I be seein' you again, Jack?

"Might be a while, Fate."

"I told you a while back that my main goal in life was to outlive that ole devil next door. Well sir, judgin' from the look on your face, I'm gonna have to find me a new reason for livin'. Guess I'll just have to hang on till you see your way back here. I'll bring ole Bandit out in a hour from now. You be careful."

The men shook hands warmly and held on for a long moment.

"Probably be some questions come morning, Fate."

"I ain't seen hide nor hair, boy," Fate said with a sly grin.

At 10:15, Jack pulled into the clearing that Fate had shown him off the Pocket Road. At the back of the clearing, behind a copse of poplars, there was an opening in the brush large enough to hide the truck from the view of passing cars. Jack parked and stepped out into the cold, bright night.

The wind had died down considerably, coming in intermittent surges between the long, still silences settling on the land. The huge moon that hung close enough to touch directly overhead in the starry sky washed the countryside in cold silver light.

Jack saw the beginning of the trail, just behind the clearing to his left. He slipped the rucksack on his back and took the ax from the bed of the truck, then listened to the night for a minute. When he was satisfied that he was completely alone he walked to the head of the trail.

Thirty yards down the trail, the land began to slope slightly toward the unseen valley below. Fifty yards farther, the trail dropped sharply and began a series of steep switchbacks. The loose gravel underfoot made for treacherous going in some places, forcing Jack to use the ax as a walking stick for balance.

Twenty minutes into his descent, he came to a clearing that offered an unobstructed view of the valley below. A hundred campfires burned in a field beside the massive stone church. Tents, pitched all around, gave the appearance of an encampment of Legionaires laying seige to a fortress. The moonlight reflected in the chrome and windows of row upon row of cars and trucks in the over-flowing parking lot. The faithful gathered to hear the final plan, Jack thought.

The trail became steeper once he passed the clearing. Jack found himself clinging to trees and shrubs for balance. Once he fell and slid for ten feet before catching hold of a pine sapling.

A half hour after he had started, Jack came to the fork in the trail that Fate had described to him. He bore to the left and came to a large boulder beside the trail some fifty yards from the fork. Knowing that he was close to the cave, he stopped and listened for a while.

The luminous hands on his watch read 10:55. Bandit should be kicking off the show any time, he thought. He climbed the boulder and settled in to wait. When he looked to his left, he saw the tip of the cross rising just above the treetops a hundred yards below him.

At the stroke of 11:00, the frenzied sound of a chorus of deep-throated hounds, baying in unison, shattered the stillness of the night. Jack climbed down to the ground and opened the pack. He removed the Mac 10 and attached the silencer and popped in a clip, then tied down the back flap and slipped the pack onto his back. He secured the ax under his left armpit so that the handle

194

stuck out behind him and the head lay face down and flush between his biceps and chest. With the little weapon held at close port arms, he moved quietly down the trail.

Twenty-five yards past the boulder, the trail switched back hard to the right. Twenty yards farther, a hard switchback to the left exposed the end of the trail at the edge of the grassy terrace where the wooden cross was planted. There was no one on the terrace.

Jack walked slowly toward the terrace, placing one foot completely down before he raised the other. When he reached the end of the trail, he squatted and listened for awhile. The only sound was the frantic music of the hounds alternating between mournful bays and staccato barks.

A dark blanket covered the entrance to the cave from the narrow opening at the top to the yard-wide passageway six feet below at ground level. Jack skirted the back of the terrace and approached the cave from the left side. A muffled voice echoed from the entrance. He leaned the ax against the boulder face and pushed the blanket three inches to the right with his left hand.

At the back of the cave thirty feet away, Reverend Clyde knelt in the middle of a circular red rug, facing the eight-foot rock wall that formed the cave's rear boundary. A circle of floating wick candles in large, oil-filled crystal bowls hung four feet off the ground, suspended by rope baskets attached to the roof of the cave. The candles hung above the perimeter of the rug and bathed the white-robed figure of Reverend Clyde in dancing saffron light. His shadow loomed large upon the rear wall.

Jack strained to hear the words that echoed softly

on the walls of the long, narrow cave. Suddenly, Reverend Clyde threw his arms above his head and raised his basso profundo voice in a litany of unintelligible phrases, filling the cave with powerful vibrations. Jack stepped inside and slipped the pack from his back, placing it against the inner wall of the entranceway. He put the Mac 10 beside it and slid the shovel from its loop.

Slowly, he crossed the sandy floor toward Reverend Clyde, whose voice continued to rise emphatically as he uttered long strings of words in the unknown language. When he reached the edge of the carpet, Jack stopped and studied the back of the white-haired figure in front of him.

The strange words began to have a physical effect on Jack, penetrating his flesh and chilling his blood. The longer he stood watching the old man, the more difficult it became to step into the circle of lights. Finally, Reverend Clyde fell silent and lowered his head.

The silence somehow released Jack's body. He stepped onto the rug and stood directly behind Reverend Clyde. His shadow on the wall, visible from the waist up, assumed the appearance of wings from the up-raised arms of Reverend Clyde, creating the illusion of some mythical half-bird, half-man creature.

A long, plaintive howl arose outside the cave, joined quickly by the voices of the remainder of the dog pack. Reverend Clyde raised his head and gasped when he saw the shadow on the wall.

"B-e-e-l-z-e-b-u-b!" he hissed. "So you have come at last. Have you come to tempt me or to beg for your chosen people? Too late, Satan! God has passed a terrible judgment on your black worshipers. He has proclaimed them a failed race and ordered me to root out their strain from the face of the earth. What say you to that, Oh Dark One?"

"Nothing."

"Then what have you come for?"

"I've come to hear you howl like the rest of the dogs."

Reverend Clyde slowly lowered his arms and turned his head to look behind him. His mad blue eyes widened when he saw Jack. When he opened his mouth to speak, Jack swung downward with the shovel, striking him on the right temple with the flat side. Reverend Clyde dropped like a stone.

Jack walked quickly to the front of the cave and removed the nylon cord from the rucksack. Reverend Clyde was moaning softly and his eyes were fluttering when Jack returned to him. Jack rolled the old man onto his stomach and bound his hands behind him, then tied his ankles together.

In the pulpit, the old man had appeared gaunt but solid. In reality, his withered flesh hung like brittle parchment from his bones. Jack doubted that he weighed more than 140 pounds. But every ounce is evil, he thought as he looked down upon Smiley's real murderer. In disgust, he turned and walked to the entrance of the cave and collected his things.

Outside the cave, the still, frigid air resounded with the song of the hounds. Jack grabbed the ax and walked down to the grassy terrace. Below him, the fires of the faithful were dying out. Above him, the radiant moon had begun its descent into the western sky. Before him stood the tall wooden cross, illuminated with such clarity by the moonlight that he could see the grain of the oak. For a long moment, he considered the cross and what he was about to do. Then, he raised the ax high above his head and swung downward at the base of the cross.

CHAPTER 25

At 7:00 Sunday morning, Darrell Day was working on his second bourbon and coffee, mixed half and half in a large cup. He sat unshaven and unwashed in his bathrobe on a stool at the kitchen counter. At the end of every fourth or fifth beat his heart was seized by a mild constriction, as if a small boa had taken up coiled residence around the laboring muscle.

The poison of thirty years association with the lowlife element had finally seeped into the deepest recesses of his soul, sullying the last pure region of his being. Cynicism had gathered like rust upon him and now threatened to freeze him into a depression from which no oil of redemption could free him.

It had all caught up. The betrayal by the Bureau that he had loved and served. The failure of his marriage. The alienation from his children. Now Courtney's death. It was too much.

He knew as he sat there that he had to make a change or die. Had to find some peace. Maybe it wasn't too late. He could sell the house and everything he owned. Maybe move to the islands. Live on his pension. Have a little fun. It seemed so simple that he couldn't believe that the thought had never before crossed his mind. The more he thought about it, the better he felt. That's it, he decided. He was toasting the idea with a neat Maker's Mark when the doorbell rang.

Darrell opened the door and found Jack Lee

slumped against the door frame. His copper curls were plastered down on his skull. The pale blue eyes were dead in their sockets in his ashen face. Blood and dirt clung to his shirt sleeves and grime caked on his jeans from the knees down.

"Jesus Christ, Rhett! You look the way I feel. Get in here."

Jack took two steps into the house and staggered. Darrell took the duffel bag from his shoulder and threw an arm around his waist. He led Jack into the kitchen and sat him down on a stool, then poured four fingers of bourbon into a water glass.

"Drink this," he commanded.

Jack tossed off the whiskey and held out the glass for another.

"I'm not sure I want to hear this one, Rhett," Darrell said as he handed Jack a full glass.

"I'm not up to telling it anyway. Do you know what station Tom Doyle works for?"

"The TV guy? Courtney's old . . . ? Yeah, I know what station, why?"

"I called him at 5:30 this morning and gave him a news tip. Figured he deserved at least that much. Point me toward a shower and go turn on the tube."

Darrell led Jack into the guest bathroom and laid out fresh towels. When Jack stripped to the waist, Darrell saw the soiled bandage on his chest and dug a small first aid kit out of the closet.

"I'll be in the den. You gonna be all right?"

"Yeah. I'll be out in a few minutes."

Jack threw his clothes into the shower and climbed in unsteadily. He turned on the water and adjusted it to the highest tolerable temperature, then aimed the stream at the back of the tub and sat down with his head lowered into the hot needles of water.

After several minutes he rose to his feet and washed himself mechanically. His mind clung to the thought that it was finally almost over. Just put one foot in front of the other until the end of the day, he thought. Then you can rest.

By the time he had dried off, changed his bandage, and put on the clean clothes from the duffel bag, Jack felt only half dead. He walked to the kitchen and poured a fresh drink, then joined Darrell in the den.

Darrell was sitting in a large easy chair in front of the television. An evangelist in a polyester suit filled the screen, whining for donations in a tear-choked voice. Darrell motioned Jack to a long sofa.

"So you called Tom Doyle, huh?"

Before Jack could answer, the evangelist disappeared from the screen and a voice announced that the program was being interrupted for a special live newscast. The image of several hundred people standing in a field with their backs to the stone Church of the Swift Sword filled the screen.

People were pointing and gesturing upward to something in front of them. The flashing blue lights of several police cars strobed in the background. Over the beating rotors of a helicopter, a voice began to describe the scene.

"This is Tom Doyle in the skylink news chopper reporting live from Sugar Valley, Georgia. Parents are warned that some of the upcoming footage contains material unsuitable for children.

"We are hovering above the scene of what appears to be the fifth in a series of bizarre murders that have occurred in the last nine days. Below us is the large congregation that had gathered this morning to hear the Reverend Clyde Causey, pastor of the white supremacist Church of the Swift Sword, relay God's final plan for America as allegedly told to Reverend Causey by God himself. Instead, these people were greeted this morning with a horrible scene, which we will show you now. Once again, be warned that children may find this scene disturbing."

The camera left the crowd outside the church and panned slowly to the right as the helicopter made a 180 degree turn. Midway through the turn, the camera caught and momentarily held the figure of an old man in overalls standing near the end of a rock promontory, a pack of black and tan hounds at his feet. The old man's face seemed impassive until the camera zoomed in and held an extreme close-up. At close range, a merry twinkle danced in his startling green eyes.

Finally, the camera moved up the side of the mountain and stopped on the wasted body of the Reverend Clyde Causey hanging from a wooden cross on a grassy terrace. His hands and feet were fixed to the cross with large nails. The skin of his body, nude except for a heavily stained pair of undershorts, was blue tinged. His head had fallen forward against his chest, exposing a crown of human ears, strung on a length of rope.

When the camera zoomed in on Reverend Clyde's head, Darrell Day counted the ears on the rope. There were ten. He looked closely and saw that Reverend

Clyde's ears were still attached. He closed his mouth, which had involuntarily dropped opened and thought back to the night at Clint DuBois's house. Yes, he was sure of it. There had been only eight ears on the rope that night. As the realization that Clint DuBois's ears had been added to the rope dawned on him, Darrell turned his head slowly toward Jack.

"God damn, Rhett, you . . . "

Darrell stopped in mid-sentence when he saw that Jack had fallen into a sound sleep. He switched off the TV with the remote and sighed deeply as he sunk back into his chair. His boggled mind shifted into neutral and idled, thoughtless and blank. When a mild cramp gripped his heart, he woke to find tears flowing silently down his cheeks. Quietly, he rose and walked from the room.

***

Jack woke in the dead silent room and kept his eyes closed until his mind was fully clear. As he lay still and felt the rhythm of his breath, he became aware of the presence of another person in the room. He turned his head and saw the hazy figure of a man bathed in the sunlight streaming into the room through partially opened Venetian blinds.

"Hello, Yeats."

"Jack."

"How long have you been standing there?"

"Oh, I don't know. A while."

"You know?"

"Yes. And for once in my life I'm speechless. I knew when I saw it on television. I hope you don't mind my coming. I was worried."

"Not at all, Yeats. It's good to see you."

"Is there anything I can do? Anything you need?"

"No. But thanks for asking. I haven't been trying to avoid you. It just seemed better to wait until all this was over."

"Then it is finished?"

"Finished."

"What now, Jack?"

"There's a lady I need to see. I haven't thought much beyond that."

"Deborah?"

"Yes."

"She called me yesterday. She's been worried sick about you, Jack."

"What did you tell her?"

"I told her that you were a survivor. That you loved her. To have faith."

"Thanks. What time is it?"

"A little after 2:00."

"Guess I should go see her now."

Jack rose from the couch and faced Yeats Murphy. There was pain and concern in the older man's face.

"I don't expect you to understand this, Yeats. I don't understand it myself."

"I don't need to understand anything. I'm just glad you're OK, lad. It's a funny thing, I've found myself praying for the first time in many years. It actually felt pretty good. I'll be praying that things go well with your lass."

The two men embraced and walked arm in arm from the room. They found Darrell Day sitting out by the patio. He had shaved, showered, and dressed in gray slacks and a blue wool sweater. A glass of Maker's Mark over ice sat in front of him on the table. A near empty bottle stood beside an ice bucket and two empty glasses.

"Sit down and join me in a drink, gentlemen," Darrell said, motioning to the two empty chairs on either side of him.

"I'll be taking my leave now," Yeats said. "You'll call me before you leave town, Darrell?"

Darrell nodded. Yeats turned to Jack and placed his hands on his shoulders.

"And you'll come in and have dinner with me sometime soon?"

"Without fail. I'll call you in a couple of days," Jack said.

Jack watched Yeats Murphy walk away. When he turned the corner of the house, Jack sat down and poured a drink.

"Hope you didn't mind me telling him you were here," Darrell said. "He was damned worried."

"No problem. What's this about you leaving town?"

"Mark it down, Rhett. This is the one that did me in. I've had it. Tomorrow this house goes up for sale. By the end of the week I'm off to find a place in the sun."

"Any place special in mind?"

"A friend of mine told me about an island. Dominica. No cruise ships. Friendly natives. A lot of rare flora and fauna. It even has some virgin rainforest. Sounds good for starters. How about yourself?"

"I don't know. A few days ago I had a lot of plans. Now . . . "

"Let me give you some advice. Don't stay in the line of fire as long as I did. Just walk out of here and find something that makes you happy. Let the world go to hell."

Jack looked closely at Darrell and saw that the fire had gone out of his black eyes. His face had softened and his once tense body had relaxed.

"Sounds like fair advice, Darrell. One last question—did your friends clean up Clint DuBois's place?"

"It's taken care of. The clean up crew found fifteen grand on DuBois's body. I told my associate to divide it among them. Kind of a bonus."

"That would have been the money that my friend paid for a sample of the herb."

They sat and drank quietly for a few minutes. Each man was aware that there was really nothing left to say. When he had finished his drink Jack broke the silence.

"Well, G-man, I guess I should be moving on. I've got a couple of people to see before dark. Thanks for all."

"Goes both ways. I don't think I could have walked away without seeing this thing settled. I said it before, Rhett, you're a real piece of work. That doesn't quite cover it, but it'll have to do. Good luck."

They stood and shook hands. It was a good handshake, warm and solid.

"I'll see myself out after I grab my things from the bathroom. I'll lock the door behind me."

"Don't bother. If you're ever in the islands . . . "

"Sure. Adios."

CHAPTER 26

Jack stopped at a pay phone and called the Thin Man. Lucy answered breathlessly on the tenth ring.

"Is that you, Jack? Are you all right?"

"I'm fine, Lucy. Is Thin around?"

"Yes, he's out in the gazebo reading. Said for you to come over anytime."

"See you in twenty minutes."

When Jack pulled around the back of Thin's house, he was greeted by the sight of Lucy, wearing a sleeveless red sun dress and high top tennis shoes, bent over a flower bed planting pansies.

"Isn't this weather something?" Lucy called out. "Twelve degrees one night and fifty-five the next day. Go on back. He's waiting for you."

Jack smiled at Lucy and walked back to the gazebo. The Thin Man, dressed in a black jump suit, sat in a deck chair reading *Pudd'nhead Wilson* by Mark Twain. A large tea pot, covered by a quilted cozy, and two cups sat on a tray on the table beside him.

Thin looked up sharply at Jack and motioned him to the deck chair on the other side of the table. He closed the book and pursed his lips, a pensive look upon his long face.

"I saw the news this morning, Jack. I'm not easily shocked, but I must say I was astounded. I always said that you were the only person I knew who was as far out there as I was. I may have understated the case."

"I trust that your sensibilities were not TOO shaken, Thin."

The Thin Man turned to Jack and smiled exposing his tiny, pearl white teeth. His far away eyes swirled like deep whirlpools of brownish yellow water in their recessed sockets.

"No, not TOO. Did you walk away clean?"

"I think so. How did things go with you?"

Thin reached down beside him and produced a small black briefcase. He placed it on the table and slid it across to Jack.

"I got eighteen for them. There were 117 pounds. Add that to the ten that I bought Friday and subtract 127 from the original 140—you get thirteen. I figure that was water loss from the extra days drying. The dollar figure comes to $210,600. It's all there in the case."

"The original deal was you keep half, Thin."

"You said Smiley had two kids. By the time they're grown, that will barely get them through college. I don't need the money. Give it to Marge."

"Seems like all I've done lately is say thanks, Thin. She'll appreciate it. So do I."

"Por Nada, Jack. I was glad to be of help."

Jack rose and offered Thin his hand.

"If you're ever in need, Thin, I expect you to call. Guess I better get this where it belongs."

Thin reached up from his chair and clasped Jack's hand firmly with his bony fingers.

"Don't be a stranger, Jack."

Lucy met Jack at the truck.

"Is everything going to be OK, Jack?"

"Everything is going to be fine, Lucy. You take care

of Thin. He's a good man."

"Always, Jack. You come back and see us soon. Thin really likes you. We both do."

"The feeling's mutual. I'll see you soon."

Jack held out his hand to Lucy. Lucy started to accept it, then gathered Jack in a powerful bear hug that left him almost breathless.

"Take care of yourself, Jack," the strange giant said as he released him.

Jack shook his head and smiled affectionately at the man in the red dress before climbing into his truck.

* * *

Jack felt a mixture of relief and anxiety when he saw Deborah's car parked in the driveway of her house on Elizabeth Street. He took several deep breaths before picking up the briefcase and getting out of the truck. A shadowy movement in the front window of her apartment caught his eye as he walked across the yard. He walked around to the back of the house and took the stairs two at a time.

As he lifted his hand to knock, the door flew open. The fine features of Deborah's face were drawn into a tight mask and her hazel eyes were filled with accusation and something else that Jack could not quite comprehend.

"It was you, wasn't it, Jack?" she asked, a tone of bitter indictment in her voice.

Jack stood silently before her.

"My God, Jack. How could you do something like that? I thought I knew you but I didn't know you at all. Not if you could do something like THAT!"

Jack took a step toward the doorway. Deborah

recoiled, eyes wide and filled with the fear that Jack had been unable to recognize a few moments earlier. The fear was deep and unreasoning and he was the object of it. It was a fear that could not be gentled, that would admit to no remedy. In a single instant the grief of loss passed through him and was replaced by acceptance. He saw clearly that they were from such different worlds, that there was neither basis nor hope for understanding between them. There was no explanation that she could accept, and even if she could accept an apology, he had none to make. It was a clear case of reality killing a dream.

They stood silent, staring at the ruin in each other's eyes. Then she eased the door closed until only her face was framed in a small crack.

"Just go away, Jack," she said as she pushed the door gently closed.

A feeling of fatalism washed over Jack as he stared at the closed door. He knew that the inevitable had occurred and that the moment was kinder now than it would have been had it come farther down the road. Every step down the back stairs reaffirmed that belief.

***

The first hint of dusk was falling when Jack pulled into Smiley's driveway. Marge's face appeared in the kitchen window as he stepped from the truck. She met him on the side deck and led him by the hand into the house.

The television in the living room was on. Two men, one dark and craggy, the other fair and smooth-faced, stood outside a large stone church. The dark-haired man held a microphone.

"This is Tom Doyle with special agent Tommy Dalton of the Georgia Bureau of Investigation. Agent Dalton, what can you tell us about the status of your investigation into these brutal murders?"

"At the present time we are in the process of evaluating information and developing leads."

"Does this mean that you do have some leads at this point?"

"I'm sorry but I can't comment further about this ongoing investigation at this time."

Jack walked over and turned the set off. A deep silence that he felt reluctant to break fell over the room. He stood and watched the setting sun paint the river with beams of gold and red. After a long while, Marge spoke.

"I'm glad that man's dead. I know it's a terrible thing to say, but I'm glad. I'm sorry though, that you . . . "

Jack turned and faced Marge.

"Don't be, Marge. It's over. If you still want to know what happened, I can tell you now."

Marge nodded and moved to the sofa. Jack put the briefcase on the coffee table and sat close beside her. She took his hand and looked into his face with misty dark eyes.

"I want to hear it all, Jack," she said quietly.

Marge listened without interruption while Jack spoke. When he finished, she leaned back and closed her eyes. There was a look of something like peace there when she opened them again.

"It helps to know. I don't know why, but it does. I'll never feel the same about the world again, but I'll get through it now. Not knowing had a strange effect on me, Jack. It was like the world had suddenly become a dangerous, uncertain place full of monsters hidden under every rock, behind every bush, just waiting to jump out unexpectedly and do horrible violence. Knowing that this was the work of insane, twisted men puts it all back in perspective."

"I'm glad, Marge. You deserve whatever peace you can find."

"What about you, Jack? Have you seen Deborah?"

Jack nodded and remained silent.

"And?"

"And nothing, Marge. There's nothing to say."

"Oh my God! You told her?"

"She figured it out. Let's just leave it there, Marge."

Marge leaned back and covered her face with her hands. Jack put his arm around her shoulders and rocked her gently back and forth until she resisted the motion and sat up straight. She turned to him and gave him a little smile. It wasn't much of a smile but it was a start, a gesture that spoke of resilience and hope.

"There is one more thing that I'd like for you to do, Jack. I think we have just enough daylight left."

Marge walked to the mantle over the fireplace and took down the silver urn containing Smiley's ashes. Jack picked up the briefcase and walked over to her. He took the urn from her and handed her the briefcase.

"You go put this in a safe place. I'll go get the boat started."

He walked down behind the house to the narrow slough where Smiley kept his little aluminum bateau and cranked the small outboard kicker. Marge arrived momentarily and slipped the line from the metal stake on the bank. She climbed into the boat and took the urn from Jack, then sat with her arms wrapped around it, on the front bench seat.

Jack eased the bateau into the river and motored upstream slowly. When they had traveled a quarter mile or so, he brought the boat about and cut the engine. The sinking sun set the river afire as it stood framed in the distance between the trees. As they drifted with the current, the sun dropped directly into the river ahead of them, transforming the water into a shimmering amber ribbon.

Marge stood when the boat began to draw even with the house. She removed the lid from the urn and turned to look at Jack. The look on her face was so fierce that it curled the hair on the back of his neck. He nodded to her and watched as she cast Smiley's ashes into the water directly in front of the house.

The white ash floated alongside the boat for a few seconds, then dispersed in the running current and was absorbed. Marge stared into the water for a long time before speaking.

"Take us home, Jack," she said quietly.

They walked back to the house with arms wrapped about each other's waists. When they reached the back steps, Marge stood on tiptoe and kissed Jack lightly on the cheek.

"I think I need a little time alone now," she said.

"Me too. I'll be in touch soon."

"There are some things I'd like to say but not right now . . . Maybe later."

"Maybe later, Marge. Come here."

They embraced and stood in each other's arms for

a long moment, then separated. Jack watched her walk quickly across the deck and enter the house. When the door closed behind her, he walked to the truck and drove away.

CHAPTER 27

Jack Lee pulled up to the gate of his driveway and turned off the engine. He sat in total darkness and breathed in the blessed silence for several minutes before stepping out of the truck and unlocking the gate. When he had driven the truck through and relocked the gate, he leaned down upon it with his elbows and cradled his head in his hands. He knew, as he stood there on the right side of the gate, that he would require nothing on the other side of it for a long time to come.

The cabin was as he had left it. He breathed in the familiar smells of home and felt profoundly comforted by its simple charm. Within minutes, a fire roared and crackled in the fireplace. Jack went into the kitchen and found the quart jar of moonshine that Fate DeFoor had given him. He filled a water glass and returned to sit on the sofa in front of the fragrant fire.

For a long while he sipped the whiskey and stared into the flames, hoping to achieve a thoughtless state leading into a deep, dreamless sleep. Each time his mind began to settle into quietude, a spur in some remote corner prodded it into restless thought. When he realized the cause of his disquiet, Jack rose from the sofa and put on a wool watchcap and gloves. Then he grabbed up his mummy bag and the jar of whiskey and stepped out onto the rear deck.

Ensconced in the deck chair beneath the warm sleeping bag, he began to work methodically on the whiskey. After a time, the barriers that he had constructed around the core of his innermost self began to fall one by one. He washed each resistance away with another swallow of moonshine until, finally, the last barrier fell and he stood revealed to himself, unguarded and unarmored. He closed his eyes and sat with himself, his true vulnerable self, for a long moment. Then, he slowly projected the events of the past week upon the screen of his mind and lingered on each image as he examined his true feelings.

When the last image faded from his mind, Jack Lee sat back exhausted and knew the truth of himself. He felt neither guilt nor remorse. Nor did he feel any particular satisfaction or gladness. At the bottom of his being there was merely contentment, a feeling of release from obligation.

Jack Lee opened his eyes and beheld the night, ready at last to say goodbye to the best friend he had ever known. As he raised his glass, a star fell in the eastern sky and blazed a fiery trail of yellow and green to the horizon. The toast that had risen to Jack's tongue served also as a wish.

"May you rest in peace, Smiley," he said aloud to the night.